FutureWord Publishing

Copyright ©2014 by Joe Vigliotti. All Rights Reserved

ISBN-13: 978-1497366305
ISBN-10: 1497366305

No part of this book may be used or reproduced, stored in a retrieval system, or transmitted in any form or by any means without prior written consent of the author, except by a reviewer who may quote passages in a review to be printed in a newspaper, magazine, or periodical; or by a reviewer electronically, such as on a website.

This is a work of fiction. However, several names, incidents, descriptions and entities included in the story are based on real people.

The opinions expressed by the author are not necessarily those of FutureWord Publishing.

Cover Artwork and Design ©2014 by Joe Vigliotti

Printed in the USA

October 2014

FutureWord Publishing
872 E. Goodman Rd. Ste. 310, Southaven, MS 38671
Fax 901-217-8514   www.futureword.net

To Nick, You are the man!

BETWEEN US AND ROME

A NOVEL OF THE LATER WESTERN EMPIRE

JOE VIGLIOTTI

To America:

Remember who you are.

This is a story of fact and fiction

They are woven together in a tapestry

The way the past and present

Form roads for posterity

ROME
April, 458 A.D.

After a half-century of invasion, war, rebellion, political corruption, and internecine conflict, the Western Roman Empire teeters on the brink of collapse. A confederation of Goth tribes under the deadly warrior lord Rufus moves to bring the other Gothic tribes under his control, and to deal the death blow to Rome. The Imperial Senate is deadlocked over a course of action. The recently-crowned Emperor Majorian seeks to defend and restore the Western Empire, but Senatorial opposition has so far hindered his efforts. While the Senate remains impotent, Emperor Majorian moves to consolidate his power to save Rome.

I

"It appears as though the crop will come in well this year."

Orianus swept his aged hand across the fledgling sprouts of wheat that had wrestled their way through the cold, muddy ground. He stood up and looked towards where his overseer, Trias, inspected the small plants several feet away. "It should be a good year," he agreed. "At least the taxes this year won't cripple the peasant farmers."

Orianus looked out across the fields, and the misty meadows, glistening with the yellow-green of early spring. There was snow, still, in the mountains, and war beyond the mountains, but here, just north of the Italian peninsula, there was safety for the time being.

"Shall we return to the villa, sir?" Trias asked. "We really shouldn't be so far away from home, or the town, without any sort of escort. It is getting dark."

"Just a few more moments," Orianus said kindly and reassuringly. He breathed in deeply, closing his eyes; the smell of wood-burned smoke was on the air, with freshly-plowed, moist earth. "How I miss this whenever the Senate reconvenes. How easily all this could be swept away." Orianus folded his arms, and turned to face Trias. "They have no idea just how tenuous things are. Gold tributes to Rufus won't keep him away forever."

Trias remained silent, contemplating what to say.

"You know you are more than welcome to speak your mind with me, Trias," said Orianus.

"Senator," Trias said at last, "we need an army. New legions. And time to grow and recover."

"Rufus will not give us that time," replied the elderly senator. "And so we must buy time with tributes. I would rather pay tribute with the sharp end of the sword."

"So would most of us," said Trias.

"Not the Senate," Orianus mused unhappily.

The sound of an approaching horse stole the attention of both men, and Trias went before his employer, sword drawn. "We should not have stayed out so long."

Through the early evening fog now emerged the rider, frantic, breathless; he dismounted in one swift movement, and bowed before Orianus.

"Senator," the man said. "Colonia Paulus burns."

Senator Orianus laid out a map over the table in the courtyard of his villa. Around him were gathered a handful of local men, trusted confidantes, and the commander of the local militia auxiliary, Tertius. Slaves brought the gathering of Romans food and drink, but no one ate or drank.

"If Colonia Paulus is razed," said Orianus, extended his finger to the northern boundaries of the Italian peninsula, "then Rufus has sent raiders into our sacred territory, through the mountain passes of the Alps."

"What of the mountain cohorts?" Tertius inquired.

"All but one of them have been stripped away to bolster the garrisons elsewhere," Orianus explained. "It was a decision I opposed. One cohort to cover an entire mountain range full of innumerable passes and gaps, tiny villages, and farmsteads. I had to fight just for that one cohort. If they're still there."

"Sir?"

"For all we know, that entire cohort has been wiped out, and nothing stands between us the barbarian hordes, except undefended land." Orianus turned to Tertius. "Have you sent out riders?"

"They'll reach the mountains in half a day," Tertius said. "And as you requested, I have also sent word under your official seal to the Emperor, to recall the Senate early."

"Good man, Tertius," said Orianus.

"Sir," said another man, standing slightly off to the side.

"Yes, Vitus?"

"Sir," said Vitus, the prefect of the nearby farming town of Tivorus, "we have received word from the prefects of other local towns that there is also an influx of refugees, from the mountains, as well as beyond. Thousands of them."

"Thousands?" asked Tertius.

Vitus nodded. "I don't want to say it, because I am a Christian, but we will be overrun and unable to help them."

"Right," said Orianus. "I, too, am a member of the Catholic Church. So we as Christians must do all that we can. Send word in all directions, to all towns and farms, to the governor, to send what can be spared to our northern regions."

"Sir," said Tertius. "There are no major towns before ours. They'll come here."

"Then have word sent to the refugees that they are welcome here."

"I'll handle that," said Vitus. "That, and sending out word for supplies. Foodstuffs and medicine."

"And I'll rally the town militia," said Tertius. "That way, we can keep order, and do what we can if there are Goths on the heels of the refugees."

The oil lamps lit up the darkness around him, a soft, yellow glow that bathed the walls and the scrolls and the pages of the study. Arrayed around him were the legal and philosophical texts that he had grown up with, an expanded collection of his father's, full of history and thought and justice and the word of God. The knock at the door was unheard at first; and thereafter, a dull thud to the clamor of Plato's Republic and the speeches of Cicero. Then, there was the voice of Vibiana, head free servant, not slave.

"Senator Servius, are you awake?"

The young man of thirty turned from the Republic to the door. "I am."

"Sir," Vibiana said. "Sir, something is going on. And there is a messenger here from Senator Orianus."

Instantly, Alban Servius was up from his desk and through the door. Both he and Vibiana strode swiftly through the corridor to the courtyard. Servius's villa was of moderate size for all the family's wealth, though his father had divested himself of much fortune in Christian pursuits such as charity. Compared to the majesty of other villas, Servius's villa could be considered merely a large farming stead –though one with much more culture and sophistication. "We are of the people," Alban's father once said, "and we should never forget that we are no better than they."

Servius met the messenger in the courtyard, who at once knelt before the approaching senator.

"No need for that," Servius said kindly. "I'll ask Vibiana to bring you some food and some water." On cue, Vibiana left for the kitchens.

"Senator Servius," said the messenger. "I thank you for your hospitality, but I do not have time to stay long. Senator Orianus to the southeast sends word that we have been notified of the destruction of the town of Colonia Paulus, most likely by raiders from Rufus's confederation. He wishes you to come to Colonia Caesarium, to his villa once you have the situation settled."

"The situation?" Servius asked.

"Yes, sir. The situation. We also have word that thousands of refugees are headed south. They may or may not pass this far west, but they are headed in the direction of Colonia Caesarium."

Vibiana returned with a pitcher of water, and cups. The messenger gladly took some water, though he passed on a roll.

"Sir," he continued, "we need anything you can spare. Food, medicine, even weapons. Work with the local prefects, the local villages, do anything you can to round up supplies. And send word to the local military auxiliaries to call up their men. Senator Orianus wishes as well for me to remind you that, though you have just been confirmed to the Senate and have yet to serve in session or be sworn in, you must use your influence as a senator in every way that you can. We need to avoid a crisis."

"I understand," said Servius. "Please let him know that I'll join him at Ceasarium with everything I can gather together, and that I'll demand the auxiliaries be put on alert."

"Very good, sir," said the messenger, and left quickly.

"Well," said Vibiana. "You know your household staff will help."

"Thank you," said Servius. "I suppose we should begin at once."

"Oh, and there's another thing, speaking of refugees," said Vibiana.

"What is it?"

"There's a girl, here, about eighteen. Her face has been cut up and bruised badly on one side. She became separated from those refugees, and somehow ended up this way. We've already taken her in."

"Where is she from?" asked Servius.

"Gaul," said Vibiana.

"Dear God," Servius said. "I knew the refugee situation was difficult. But I had no idea they were coming from Gaul, too. That's the furthest north we've ever had."

"Well," said Vibiana in a motherly tone, "when you get to Rome, do something about it."

The refugees began arriving in Colonia Caesarium just before dawn, in small groups, then as a trickle, then as a solid stream. Senator Orianus donned his old battle armor, the regalia of a former legion

16

commander, and rode out with members of the town militia to stand among the road to see the people in. The panic prevalent among many of the refugees was calmed considerably by the sight of a Roman soldier who welcomed them and reminded them to keep in good order, as good Romans do.

By midmorning, the refugees had mostly stopped coming, and Orianus decided to return to the town. "How many have come in?" he asked one of the militiamen that had ridden out with him.

"More than a thousand," was the reply.

"And the Goths?"

"One of the refugees, the assistant to the prefect who organized the procession away from Colonia Paulus, reports that the Goths have returned to the other side of the mountains."

Orianus sighed happily. "There, at least, is one issue temporarily abated. Nevertheless we must be cautious. Send out two more riders north to ascertain the situation. Have them see about the messengers we sent to the garrison as well."

"Yes, sir!"

Orianus urged his horse along, toward the town as another messenger came riding up.

"Senator," the man said. "The surrounding communities are sending what they can. Some supplies and foodstuffs have already reached the town. More is arriving. The governor sends his respects, and promises martial support if needed, but he says he cannot send any supplies from the garrison cohort there. Sir, they've stripped his supplies to send to the Spanish front."

"As expected," Orianus shook his head. "Very well."

As the messenger departed, another arrived.

"Sir," said the messenger. "I am Horatio, overseer from the estate of Senator Servius. He sends his respects, and will be accompanying a caravan of supplies later this day."

"Thank you, Horatio," Orianus replied as the man returned across the fields toward home.

Tertius and an aide rode out of town as Orianus and his group neared. "Everything is in hand," Tertius reported, his old armor glinting in the sunlight. "Our men are armed, and are ready for any trouble. But there isn't any trouble to be had. The people are happy to know they are under your protection, now."

"Good," said Orianus. "See to it that the supplies are stockpiled and rationed carefully. And see to it that messengers are sent to the other villas. There are a few other senators brave enough to live this far north. Prevail upon them if they are so inclined to aid our project here."

"With pleasure, sir." Tertius turned to his aide to dispatch him.

"And what of shelter," Orianus inquired. "Has that been seen to?"

"Of course the inn is full," said Tertius. "We've secured a number of tents, and some lumbermen are preparing some makeshift structures around the outskirts of town. Senator Celsus is shipping north to us a supply of military tents, which were mistakenly shipped on loan to him last week from the governor. Senator Celsus wanted pavilion tents for his local fair. He should be lucky they didn't send him elephants."

"Thank God for small favors," Orianus commended. "We should move into town, now. And speak to the people themselves. They are refugees, of course; but they are people."

"I'll never understand your Christian worldview, sir," said Tertius. "Give me the bloody gods of old."

"God," Orianus observed, "is love and peace and forgiveness. But I have learned this from my studies of the Christian texts: do not cross Him."

"We need an angry God," said Tertius. "Although, I would be happy with a Senate full of fire and out for blood." Tertius gritted his teeth and rapped a fist against his chest armor. "Just once, to be back on the battlefield, to be thirty again, or twenty…"

"If Rufus and his Gothic thugs cross over the mountains and stay next time, you'll get your chance, my old friend," Orianus said consolingly.

As they rode through the plaza of the town, the refugees —who sat huddled amongst themselves, mostly silent, their families and their lives in shambles —looked up to Orianus; many of them stood and began to gather around him. Some looked angry. Some looked terrified. Some looked as though they may fall apart with the slightest breath of wind.

What to say to them, he wondered. What to say to people whom had lost everything? Though Orianus was an old man, years on the field of battle —and in the halls of the Senate —had given his voice tremendous strength. Sitting straight in the saddle, he spoke to the people.

"Romans," he said. "This is Colonia Ceasarium. This is my home, and you are welcome here. I am Senator Orianus, and I have made the surrounding officials and towns aware of your condition. As we speak, help is pouring in from every possible stretch of the northern regions. I ask that while you are here, you show good order, and keep that order. We are the civilized people of the world, and we conduct ourselves with integrity and honor, no matter what sacrifices we have endured." He breathed in deeply; the people – almost all of them –were listening.

"You may stay here for as long as you require," he said. "I'm not sure what can be done in the way of permanent lodging, and I must be honest. We can't afford to keep you for long without your help. If you choose to remain here, and not to return to Colonia Paulus, we ask that you pay for your keep by assisting with our local economy. We are looking for men for the militia. Farmers always could use the help plowing their fields and sowing crops. Tradesmen are looking for apprentices. The wealthier households always seek good maids and workers. The same is true for our neighboring towns and villages."

Orianus paused. There was silence among the people around him. Now, everyone was paying attention. Words formed on their lips, but no one had the courage –or the strength –to say anything. Orianus removed his helmet.

"Please," he said. "I am here to understand. What is it you wish to say?"

Silence. Tense silence.

Just as Orianus was about to continue, a monk – his face bloodied and untended –stepped forward. He clutched a rosary in his hand.

"Sir," said the monk. "My name is Marcellus. I was born in Rome, and I serve the mountain towns. May I have your permission to speak?"

Orianus dismounted his horse, handing the reigns to Tertius. "You have it."

"Senator," Marcellus went on. "We have traveled a ways to get here. Colonia Paulus is razed. I am afraid we cannot go back. The people have elected me to speak for them, so I do so as humbly, justly, and as forthrightly as God can give me means to do. I thank you for your gift of stay here. I am sure I speak for all when I say that your kindness is far greater than anything anyone could have expected. And we will always be grateful for it. We will not be idle, especially those of us whom stay on." The monk held a hand up to his face, as if to ward off the sheer amount of pain that Orianus knew he must be enduring.

"Sir, the one question that is on everyone's mind, is what is to be done." He quickly added, "not just for vengeance, but to protect the thousands and thousands of other innocents that will suffer a similar injustice at the hands of the Goths."

The airing of this grievance brought out the bravest of the people. Voices rang out, demanding to know where the Roman legions had been, why the Senate was stripping away the transalpine garrisons, why the tax rates had not been lowered for the region to handle the costs of the raids —and the questions went on.

Orianus raised his hands. "Romans," he called. "Hear me. Know that I have understood your plights, and I will address them in the Senate."

"The Senate is corrupt!" came the response.

"The Senate will not help us!" came another voice.

"Burn the Senate!" shouted a third.

"Well," said Orianus, "hopefully I shall not be in the Senate if it comes to that."

The response was disarming, and several people laughed. The crowd began to settle down as Orianus took to horseback once more.

"Friends," he addressed them. "The Senate is a war in and of itself. But know that I have heard you. I, and other senators in this region have seen firsthand the poor policies of the Senate. And we will not let you down. I leave for Rome tomorrow, to see the Emperor himself."

"Then, sir," said the monk Marcellus, stepping up to Orianus's horse. "Will you remember us to him?"

Orianus nodded. "I will remember all of you to Rome herself."

The column of wagons full of supplies, with Servius at the very fore, arrived by early afternoon. The column was manned by men from the farms surrounding his estate, and they would return to their homes within a few hours. Servius, however, would not return. He was packed and prepared to journey to Rome that very day if the need arose. He had seen to everything before he left. Vibiana had been put in charge of everything. He trusted her like he had trusted his own mother, Cassia, Vibiana's best friend. Cassia had been dead for a decade, having died shortly before Servius's father.

Vibiana would see to the planting, and the irrigation ditches, and the records and accounts. Servius had turned a marginal profit yet the year before, and he was determined to do better this year with the autumn harvest. The farmers in his region had, likewise, only broken even from the toils of their own hands, and from tax breaks. There had been a shortage of foodstuffs in the last few years, with the civil wars that brought down two emperors, and put up three. The wars –in addition to invasions –had taken their toll on the economy.

As Colonia Caesarium drew near, Servius could see what Rome had once been. He could see the great, rolling green hills of the countryside laid out before him like a quilt; patches of sunlight and shadow fell across plots of freshly-plowed and planted earth. He thought of the works of Tacitus, of the agrarian roots of the world's superpower. Simple farms and small, unassuming villages had produced the mightiest force the world had ever known. If only, thought Servius, if only Rome could return to everything she once was.

But the family farm had been long and largely forgotten, somewhere among the pages of the past. Few were looking back for the foundation of the future.

As Servius and his column pulled up before Caesarium, he could see the refugees moving about in good order. From out on the country roads, Servius could see another column of supplies, perhaps tents it seemed, arriving; a handful of auxiliary troops stood on guard near what had become a storehouse. Everything was in good order. The auxiliaries saluted, and one of them came forward in standard Roman armor. It was Tertius.

"We were expecting you, Senator Servius. We are happy you're here." Tertius called for his horse, and mounted. "Your people can rest and stay as long as they need to. My men can unload the wagons, and they'll see your belongings to Senator Orianus's estate. I thank you, personally, for your quickness here."

"We were all happy to help," Servius explained as they rode toward the center of town. "I sent out a call for volunteers and supplies, and people turned out in droves to assist our effort."

"At least someone is assisting the effort," said Tertius. "I will never understand the Senate. There are not many who are just."

Servius nodded. He was well-aware of the disdain nearly all of the people in the northern regions had for the politicians in Rome. While they sweated and froze and wore out their lives in the fields and in the mountains, Rome taxed them and penalized them and regulated them and failed to protect them. Sometimes the emperors were complicit; other times, the emperors were uncaring or merely self-serving.

The most pressing issue now on Servius's mind was to ensure the protection of the north, and to defend the passes of the mountains. For this, he wanted to raise an entirely new legion of soldiers, and to put at their command General Tremissis Scipio, who had fought alongside Flavius Aetius against Attila the Hun only a few short years before. Since the civil wars, not much had been heard of Scipio, who helped lead the counterattack at Catalaunian Fields. Most believed he had retired. Servius was determined to bring him out of retirement.

The death of Aetius at the hands of Emperor Valentinian III had been unexpected and deeply felt. Aetius had become too popular in the eyes of the people, and so he was done away with. When the Emperor was attacked and assassinated later on, his guards —men who had served under Aetius —stood by and did nothing. Aetius was one of the few men capable of defending Rome in the present, and now he was gone, leaving only Scipio and Emperor Majorian.

It was Majorian who had handpicked Servius to serve in the Senate. Servius was unsure why the Emperor of Rome should see fit to select him for such a position, for he had no previous political experience, and had merely been living as a farmer, in the way of Cincinnatus. Servius was sure, however, that the Emperor would explain things to him in Rome.

Orianus was in the center of the town, surrounded by a number of men and women, including Marcellus, whose head had been carefully treated and bandaged. Recently arrived Senator Vespius, living to the northwest, had also arrived. Vespius, Orianus, and Servius's father had once formed a triumvirate in the Senate, one which worked ceaselessly to advance populist causes consistent with the laws of Rome, and sometimes in defiance of them.

Both Vespius and Servius were happy to see the arrival of Servius, who at once dismounted from his horse and proceeded to greet them.

"Servius," said Vespius, "I have not seen you since last autumn. You're looking well."

"Thank you," said Servius. "As are you."
Vespius laughed heartily. "For a fat man of sixty, I suppose I am doing quite well."

"Thank you for coming," said Orianus with a smile. "We are grateful for your assistance."

"You would do the same," Servius replied. "I hope I have not interrupted the meeting."

"Not at all. We were simply discussing with some of the town's leaders and elders their concerns, and what could be done to facilitate the needs of their people."

Servius nodded as Orianus introduced him all around, including to Marcellus.
"The reputation of your father precedes you, sir," said Marcellus kindly. "We were friends."

"You are the Marcellus he spoke of when he wrote to me from Rome," Servius said with interest. "He wrote about you helping to pull drunkards from the street, saving them from a passing chariot."

"Rome is overrun," said Marcellus. "It is one of the reasons why I left for the mountains. Nevertheless, I will be returning to the city to help press the case for stronger defenses, all within the confines of the just war credentials of Augustine of Hippo. With such authority, I don't see how any Christian could turn away."

Orianus and Vespius said nothing; most of the Senate, full of many Christians, had turned away time and time again. But, Orianus hoped, this time it would be different, for the people of Colonia Paulus were Roman citizens within the traditional realm of Rome. There would be nothing he would have to say before Majorian to convince him, for Majorian had long been decided. No, Orianus knew, the trouble would be with the Senate.

They day wore on, and the sun rose high, and bathed the land in warm light, and the fledgling crops rose toward the sky. Supplies poured in to Colonia Caesarium, and volunteers to assist the people came and went. Employers came seeking new workers, and various Catholic churches and orders came to administer to the refugees.

And Servius went among the refugees, speaking to as many of them individually as he could, taking notes on a small scroll which was rapidly being filled up. Orianus and Vespius both noticed that he sat beside them, stood with them, looked them in the eyes. It was a rare trait for a politician to look at someone, and not down on him. What was more about Servius, Orianus knew, was that he was not naïve, nor was he dishonest. He would be a rare addition to the Senate, provided he proved to be beyond corruptibility. Indeed, if Servius was anything like his father, the way that Orianus hoped, that would still be the case.

He moved among the people, just the way the Savior had. Perhaps Servius could somehow serve to be the savior of Rome, the older senator mused. The interactions Servius had with lower-level local politicians, and the people, was something altogether different. Part of it was certainly due to his father; but perhaps the larger part of it was due to the man himself.

And some nights, Orianus looked up at the sky, at the stars, and the lights twinkling in distant valley farms, and high on the mountaintops, and he wondered. He wondered about the farmers, and the peasants, and the patricians. He thought about the roads, and aqueducts, and the towers and buildings and walls, the baths and the estates, the forum and the shops, the sheer volume and scale of production and consumption and business interaction, the knowledge accumulated from the echoes of history. Sometimes it seemed as if such a world of beauty and structure and complexity would exist forever, unchanged, impregnable, indestructible, eternal. At other times, it seemed as if such a world was bound together by a single thread.

And sometimes Orianus felt as if he, too, were bound together by a single thread.

One defeat, one moment, could mean the end of everything that had been for hundreds of years.

After all, it had only been a few years since the invasions of the Huns, and the sacking of Rome herself by the Vandals. Such a thing been thought impossible in 410, the first time the great city had been sacked. The only question now was, would there be a third? And if so, would another such occurrence bring down all of the empire? Would it be a successful Hannibalian invasion?

The night had come on, and the low rumble of a spring storm echoed through the hills. Colonia Ceaserium lay quiet under the cloud-covered night sky, and a cool, humid breeze came down from the mountains. Servius sat with Orianus on the steps of his villa, perched on the crest of rise that overlooked the entire estate. Torches from the night watch in town on the horizon could be seen moving before and behind the various homes and shops, like fireflies in the summer trees.

Yet it wasn't beauty that Servius ruminated on, or described to the older senator. Servius could see the burning silhouette of Caesarium, and the ruined earth, and long trains of refugees, of Roman citizens enslaved, of the collapse of the civilized world. And Orianus listened intently, listened carefully to the things Servius said —Servius, the son of Orianus's best friend —of all the things that would be, that should be, that couldn't be. Orianus understood, as he listened, the stone of the steps cold on his hands, that Servius was more than just a good man: he would be a crucial ally in the Senate. Orianus would bring Servius into the fold, would place his trust in the young man, full of ideas and ideals; and he would bring him into league with Vespius and the other conservative senators, for the young man was himself clearly a conservative, and quite distinctly a Christian. And besides, Orianus reasoned, Majorian himself had selected Servius.

Time enough for plotting later, the old senator reminded himself, and stood stiffly. "I'm off to sleep, my young friend," he said. "Do get some rest. We have a long journey ahead of ourselves in the morning. We're going to head for the sea, and sail south to Rome."

Servius stood, and thanked Orianus for the guest quarters, but remained on the steps after the old man had gone in. He breathed in deeply, felt the night's chill, and was reminded that the warmth of summer was still far off. The lights from inside the villa burned brightly, and the luminous glow spilled across the steps like water.

"Dear God," Servius whispered to Heaven, his eyes closed. "Give me the strength to do this. Give me the strength to make this all right. I ask, Father, that you guard the innocent, and heal the hearts of those whom have been terribly hurt through this ordeal. Dear God, move the hearts of men to make wise choices."

When Servius opened his eyes, the flame and ash were gone, and there was all of Rome, all of the empire, quiet and tranquil under the dark sky once more.

II

The sun appeared beyond the horizon, stretching out toward eternity, throwing off the veil of night. By the time the fiery orb appeared fully in the sky, Orianus, Vespius, and Servius had assembled themselves for the journey to Genoa. Tertius would be accompanying them to Rome, as would a select handful of auxiliaries, to act as guards until the port.

The small party boarded a ship, along with a number of other officials, dignitaries, and important civilians bound for the capital city. The waters were busy with merchant ships, and fishing boats, and a military trireme out on exercises. Servius stood about, watching the bustling traffic, aware of just how great and intricate the affairs of the empire and its inhabitants were –and just how unaware they were of the tragedy that had befallen Colonia Paulus the day before. Soon enough, news would reach all of Italy, but not much would be done, for the north was far away, and the concerns there not a priority for the rest.

While at starboard, Servius was joined by Orianus and Vespius. The sea air, salted and fair, came dancing across the water, sending waves to lap against the hull of the ship as it headed south.

"It is a good wind," remarked Vespius. "We should reach Rome by tomorrow, if it keeps up."

Servius nodded, but his thoughts centered about the recent sacking of Rome and Aquileia, and the raid on Colonia Paulus. He had been contemplating speaking to both the older senators about the need for a new legion to defend the northern reaches of Rome, and perhaps even to act offensively against the Goths. Every single refugee he had spoken with about the matter wanted to know where the Roman troops had been. Servius decided that in the Senate, this would be his first priority. He had carefully studied Roman law and the politics of the Senate, simply to be well-informed; when the Emperor Majorian had come to his villa to press him to accept nomination to the Senate three weeks before, Servius had redoubled his efforts to understand the Curia.

Better now than in Rome, Servius thought. He breathed in sharply.

"I have been wondering," said Servius evenly, "where either of you stand on the idea of raising and equipping a new legion? This new legion to be raised so that it would, at the very least, defend the northern boundaries, and at most, take the fight to the Gauls."

Orianus and Vespius said nothing for a moment, then regarded one another with bemused expressions.

"A legion," Orianus said carefully, testing the younger senator. "A fully-armed legion."

"Yes," said Servius. "Rome is in need of many reforms. But the way I see it, we first need to defend the empire against external attempts at collapse."

"Then," Vespius said, his hands clasped before him, "the three of us are of the same opinion."

"The process," Orianus said, "will not be an easy one. When you are officially sworn in by Emperor Majorian, we will begin to form a coalition of senators around a set of ideas, among them, taking priority, mobilization for the defense of Rome. It is only a matter of time, as we all know, before Rufus returns with a larger force with more established targets. We need the resources to meet that challenge."

"We will have to remain steadfast to achieve our goals," Vespius offered casually, seeing if Servius would agree. "We must therefore not be afraid to seek victory at whatever cost."

"So we would be something of a triumvirate, an alliance," Servius offered. "An alliance like the one you both held with my father."

"Then it shall be," said Orianus.

A sailor on the ship approached the three senators, asking for Servius. "Sir," said the man, "there is something that requires your attention."

Always cautious, Orianus stepped up beside his young friend. "What is it?"

"A stowaway, sir," said the sailor.

As Servius went ahead, Vespius stayed Orianus by the arm. "He is indeed what we need," said Vespius. "Though I worry that perhaps his moral idealism will interfere with the need for his pragmatic understanding."

"There are few men left of such principle," said Orianus. Both men then continued after Servius.

In the hold below, the ship's captain, Ralla, along with one of his men, stood beside an opened crate. They didn't seem terribly concerned, but they weren't at ease, either. When Servius entered, both men bowed their heads slightly in deference.

"There's a stowaway?" Servius asked Ralla.

"Yes," said Ralla. "My man here found her attempting to steal some bread from the galley."

"What does it have to do with me?" Servius asked as Orianus and Vespius appeared behind him.

Ralla ran a hand through his hair. "It's a girl. Says she knows you. Says she was planning to follow you to Rome to meet you there. At first, I thought she might have been an assassin, but then, when I saw her, I knew better. She hasn't come out of the crate, and says she won't come out unless you ask her to. None of us had the heart to fight her out, considering her condition."

Servius approached the crate slowly, and peered in. Before him was the huddled form of a refugee, in rags once a Gallic tunic, barely covering her body. She looked up at him with wide eyes, fearful, unsure; her face was badly bruised, and her long, dark hair lay about her shoulders. At once, Servius knew who the girl must be, and he removed his cloak to cover her up. She nearly recoiled at his touch, but once his hands were away, she clutched at the material, pulling it tight around her.

"You came to my estate," he said.

The girl nodded sullenly, and the other men in the room glanced at one another, now at ease.

"I'll handle it from here, Captain," said Servius. "But perhaps you would send your ship's doctor?"

"I shall send him at once." Ralla bowed his head, and followed by his man, left the hold.

"We'll leave you to it," said Vespius, who left thereafter with Orianus.

When all four men had gone, Servius turned back to the girl before him.

"They've left," he said gently. "If you'd like, I can go, too." But somehow, he knew the girl would refuse his absence, and she did.

"What is your name?"

The girl gave no answer.

"Would you like to come out of there?" he asked.

The girl nodded, and Servius offered her his hand. She regarded it carefully at first, then gently reached out and clasped it, and he helped her up and out. He replaced the lid to the crate, and turned around so the girl could adjust the cloak around her. She then kneeled, and sat on the floor.

"Why didn't you stay at the estate?" he asked her.

The girl breathed in deeply, and she spoke. "You can turn now," she said, her voice weak and strained.

Servius turned to face her, and his heart twisted when he saw how badly her face had been battered. She was beautiful, he realized –too beautiful to have been the victim of Gothic raids. She should be home, safe with her family, and not here.

"Why didn't you remain at the estate?" he asked again, kindly.

"Because I needed to see you," she said. "I wanted to go with you to Rome."

Servius folded his arms, and leaned against a crate.

"For what purpose?"

"I am surrendering myself to you as a slave," the girl said. She appeared to be on the brink of tears. "You took me in, and I owe you my life."

Servius put his hands up. "No," he said. "I own no slaves, and I will never own a slave."

The girl trembled. "Then what is to become of me?"

"I will pay you to work as a servant," said Servius, thinking quickly. Vibiana, he knew, could use more help. The girl would then have a home, and wages, and a way to begin her life again.

The girl began crying, doing her best to bite back her tears. She pulled his cloak tighter around her shoulders, as if to steady herself. Servius was unsure what to do.

"Thank you," she whispered. "I will do anything you ask of me. Anything. But please, do not send me back."

"Well," said Servius, "I'm not sure I have much say at this moment. We're at sea." But his attempt at light humor was lost on the girl, and he scolded himself internally for it, considering everything the girl had been through.

"What about when we enter Rome?"

Servius considered the question. "It would do well to have an attendant," he said. "But, I should like your name if I am to pay you to work for me."

The girl raised her delicate, green eyes. "I am Prisca," she said.

"A Roman name," Servius said in acknowledgement.

"My father was a soldier," she explained. "He was born and raised in Rome. After his service, he journeyed to settle in Gaul, and there met my mother. She was a weaver, and my father turned to blacksmithing. And I had a younger sister…" Tears welled in her eyes once more at the memory of her now deceased parents.

"Well, Prisca," said Servius. "I am happy to know you. I wish the cause for our meeting had been different, but we have to work with the challenges we have before us."

Prisca nodded. He noticed that in her hand, she clutched a small, metal cross.

"Are you Christian?" Servius asked, kneeling beside her.

"Are you not?" Prisca asked, nervously.

Servius reached into his tunic, and withdrew his own small cross, held about his neck, and the girl no longer looked as nervous.

"My father made this for me," she said. "May I keep it with me?"

Servius nodded. "I would never dare take away such a symbol of faith, or love. You don't even have to ask me that."

Prisca nodded. "Thank you."

"When we're in Rome, we'll find a good ribbon or string for it." The suggestion met with approval by the girl. Servius looked toward the steps, wondering where the ship's physician was, unsure of what to do next, hoping to avoid an uncomfortable and tense silence.

"How old are you?" he asked.

"Eighteen," Prisca replied. "I turned eighteen last month."

"Were you ever engaged or married?"

"At sixteen, I was engaged to a boy who enlisted in the army. He promised he would come back and marry me, but he was killed while putting down an insurrection in Spain."

Prisca, Servius realized, truly was alone.

"I am sorry for that," he said at length. "I am sorry for everything that has happened." He figured it was best to turn the conversation away from personal events.

"And in what areas are you skilled?" he asked.

"I can sow crops and sew and tailor clothing. I can clean, and cook, and tend to horses. I can ride, too. I can do small amounts of smithing, as my father instructed me. And I can read, and I can write."

Servius inclined his head slightly, and smiled. "I'm impressed," he admitted. "You're certainly qualified for work."

Just as the girl looked as though she might have become comfortable, approaching footsteps stole her attention, and she drew Servius's cape about her even more tightly. Servius looked up to see the ship's physician enter.

"I'm sorry, sir," said the man. "I was attending to someone with simple sea sickness. We had been panicked it was something contagious."

"Well, doctor, I shall leave you to it." Servius stepped toward the door, and cast a quick glance back at Prisca, whose concern and fear grew with each step he took. "I'll be right outside, waiting," he explained. "We'll find you some better clothing as well."

"Senator," said Prisca as the physician brought out cloths to clean her face. "Thank you."

Servius bowed his head slightly, and headed out.

"The transalpine cohort's fate was still unknown when we left Genoa," Vespius lamented. "If that cohort is gone, there is nothing defending central northern Italy."

Senator Capito leaned forward across the table, his dinner untouched, his stomach still reeling from the afternoon's bout with sickness. "The cohort did not engage the raiders?" He steadied himself against the rocking of the ship.

"Of that we are unaware, either," Orianus said slowly, his mind drifting across the mountain passes. "You should consider yourself justified you voted against removing the full legion."

Capito took a settling sip of water, and breathed in deeply. "The sickness is mostly passed, I think. But my voting to keep the legion in place doesn't help me feel any better." Capito folded his hands, and looked at his fellow senators.

"Since the beginning of this little voyage, I have been ill. The sea always does it to me. We have fought against each other, and defended one another in the past. You have rousted me out of what I had hoped would be a last non-political trip before the Senate convenes. So please, both of you. Speak what is on your mind."

"Troops," said Vespius decidedly. "We will be pressing for an entirely new legion to defend the mountain passes."

"I have no concern about that," Capito said blandly. "I support defending the borders, but why new troops?"

"Because we are stretched to the breaking point," Vespius pressed. "We have no troops between us and the northern frontier of Italy."

"Raising a new legion, or two, or ten, will cost money," Capito said. "Suddenly, I feel slightly better."

"I had hoped you would. Your family's armory is famous for its quality of product and its loyal service to the Republic and to the Empire. What I am proposing is

39

that the contracts for arming this new legion will fall solely on the Capito manufacturers."

Capito inclined his head. "If the Emperor and the Senate called upon my smiths to produce such a vast number of weapons and materials, instead of their own state armories, we would of course oblige, happily. And for the securing of the entire contract for production of armaments, we would of course, provide the Senate with a deal, so as not to tax its coffers too greatly."

"That is what we'd hoped," said Vespius. "It would be an honor to secure you the contract –but in order to do so, we need more troops, and we need your support in the Senate."

Capito stood stiffly. "It is done," he said. "You shall have my support wherever needed. After all, the economy must be strengthened in addition to our borders." He looked both men in the eyes. "And rest assured that my cousin, Senator Culleo, will also support this effort."

"We are glad for the help," said Vespius.

Capito stopped at the door. "Don't mistake my intentions," he added as he put a hand on his stomach. "I want a profit for the armory, of course. But as a senator, I serve Rome first. And there must be a Rome left to do business with. I love Rome, like you do."

"You are as practical as you are philosophical," Vespius conceded as Capito left. He then turned to Orianus.

"When push comes to shove, he'll abandon the cause."

Orianus considered Vespius's words a moment before speaking. "Then we shall have to make sure to guarantee his cooperation with those contracts."

"There are other senators with connections who will want those contracts."

"That is true."

"Well," Vespius concluded. "We'll have to figure out what else we can leverage."

Servius stood on deck alone that night, the chilly sea air rushing across the prow of the ship. It felt more like winter than like spring, even for the Mediterranean.

Prisca had been put up with a few other female slaves, who promised to care for her through the trip to Rome. Prsica seemed to be much more at ease in their company, and Servius was grateful for it. And from behind him now approached Marcellus.

"Good evening, Senator," he said.

"Good evening, Father Marcellus."

"The girl is definitely more relaxed, though fear plagues her like disease."

Servius nodded.

"The physician explained to me her condition," said Marcellus. "She has been horribly beaten, and will require rest and care. I trust that you will not compel her to undertake any strenuous physical activity until she is well?"

"Of course not," Servius confirmed.

"The physician also explained to me that she has been violated, as well. She will require emotional and spiritual sustenance."

"Can I count on you to provide that?" Servius asked.

"I am not sure if I am the right person for the job," Marcellus conceded. "Perhaps a nun from the convent would be better."

Servius nodded once more. "I pray she recovers."

"She will as best she can, in time," Marcellus explained. "But there is still the issue of her purity, of her being."

"Speak plainly, Marcellus," said Servius.

"Marriage will not be easy, if not impossible for her. She has mentioned to me that you have agreed to hire her on as a servant in Rome. Will she continue serving you after you leave?"

"Absolutely," Servius replied without a second's hesitation.

Marcellus bowed his head slightly. "It is a Christian thing to do. And the girl will be much relieved to hear that her engagement with you will not be temporary. At the very least, she will have a home."

"You're a good man, Marcellus."

"I am a servant of God. If there is anything good in me, it is because God has touched my life."

"I certainly hope," Servius said as he cast his gaze out toward the dark horizon, "that the Senate hears what you have to say."

"I have not been to Rome in two years," said Marcellus. "I wonder what it has to say."

III

The ship landed at the mouth of the Tiber River, the outer limits of Rome, just as the sky tinged with the gray of dawn. Red-tiled roofs of homes, gleaming white columns, churches, and shops covered the landscape, and ships came in to dock in the stead of departing boats. The screech of seagulls and the lapping of saltwater against the hulls of vessels and piers comingled with the bustle of a burgeoning populace, coming and going, selling and buying, building and crafting. Servius looked over the docks, washed warmly by the bright morning sun.

"It is beautiful," Servius said to Orianus as the ship was moored.

"Rome is not what she once was," said the elder senator bitterly. "You will not like what you see past the façade. This is not our home, but a cesspool of the filth of humanity. The only thing beautiful about this place anymore is the flame, the idea. A ghost."

The younger senator nodded. "Rome has always been an idea."

"You will find Rome much changed from the days of your father, my friend," Orianus said. "And if you can still find that same hope and belief in the ghost of yesteryear, then you are a far better man than Rome deserves."

They traveled by carriage toward the city, through small farms and past villas and small hamlets, all of it a part of the outstretched hand of Rome, proper. The dawn had unveiled a clear, blue sky, speckled with bright, white clouds, tracing patterns of soft shadow and sunlight across the land.

As they crested the final hill before the city, the aqueducts and the coliseums and the marble buildings came into view. Rome stretched as far as they eye could see, spread out over the land like falling water.

Orianus watched both Servius, and the girl. If there was any excitement in his mind, Servius did not show it. His expression, his demeanor, was calm and observant. The girl, Prisca, for everything she had been through in the past forty-eight hours, was wide-eyed and watchful, fearful but impressed upon, having not seen anything like the city in her entire life. Marcellus was unimpressed; he had been to Rome before, and would return to Rome again. Vespius was sleeping; Capito had ridden ahead to meet his cousin.

Moving through the streets of the heart of the city, Orianus watched as Prisca turned her head left, and right, and up. Rome was alive. The markets were thriving. Potteries of every shape, size, color, and style lined the shelves of sellers; jewelers displayed gold and silver ornaments of every kind, embedded with gems of every color; figurines, lamps, oils, perfumes, linens and silks, housewares, religious icons and materials, sandals, belts, leather goods, trunks, furniture, grain, bread, meat, fruits, vegetables –if it could be produced, it could be traded or sold.

All around and in between the sellers were churches and the places of business of physicians and surgeons, of lawyers and architects, of cobblers and smiths and tradesmen, public baths, public cisterns for water from the aqueducts, circuses, and even houses of ill-repute. Beneath their feet ran the sewers, the pipes, the fetid waste of the city —yet the system of plumbing was a marvel of Roman ingenuity and skill, unrivaled in the world.

And from shop to shop, from home to home, from one place to the next, moved the people of Rome themselves. Men in white and gray tunics went about with their wives, daughters, mistresses, themselves dressed in pastel-colored fabrics, many of them sheer and weightless, adorned with veils and jewels and precious metals.

Servius looked at them, at the beautiful girls, and the beautiful colors, and the beautiful city in the daylight. What a people so removed, he thought; a people so removed and unaware of what was at their doorstep, just a few hundred miles away. He wondered if, even worse, they were aware, but they simply did not care, for here was Rome, and Rufus was over the Alps.

The carriages turned away from the public wells and the squares and the shops, toward Palatine Hill, above the great forum. There, the Emperor, many Senators, patricians and aristocrats lived in great houses with spacious courtyards, in palaces and in villas, dotted by churches and their crosses, stadiums and luxury shops and brothels. Members of the Emperor's Guard, patrolled the streets, and protected those who made their homes there. On Palatine Hill lived the greatest citizens of Rome, and dwelt the greatest progenitors of salvation and sin.

Servius had been appointed a grand house beside Orianus's, with a columned face, balconies, a magnificent pool in a flowered courtyard, and a servant staff of six. A young man of the Emperor's Guard, Titus, presented himself and the keys to the front gates of the house to Servius, as he and Prisca went from Orianus's home to theirs.

"Emperor Majorian has personally called upon me to be your bodyguard and your messenger," Titus explained. "As soon as we unload your carriage, I am to escort you and Senator Orianus to Emperor Majorian."

"I thank you," Servius told Titus. "This is my personal attendant, Prisca." She bowed her head to Titus, who nodded in deference.

"It is an honor to serve you, Senator," said Titus. "I spent my childhood in Milan, so the northern reaches have my heart. It is where my wife and three children live, though they are coming to Rome this week. I could not abide them being so far away, with the raids that have been going on."

"You're aware of the raids?" Servius asked as he and Titus headed toward his carriage. Next door, Orianus's staff was unloading his trunks.

"The northern regions have been prone to raids and wars for decades," Titus explained as he directed the staff to the luggage. "Now, with Rufus on the loose, that only complicates what had been a difficult situation."

Servius nodded. "Only recently have the raids moved to our region of the north."

"And forgive me," said Titus, "for being so transparent. But I know Emperor Majorian has personally appointed you to the Senate. If he sees fit to trust you, then you can be trusted, and I would lay down my life for yours, for Rome."

"On only his word?" Servius asked.

"On only his word," Titus said, bowing his head.

"Then it appears as though I have one more citizen's trust to uphold," Servius said kindly.

An elderly woman then presented herself with Titus's introduction. "I am Amica," she said. "I am the head of staff, here."

"It is good to know you," Servius said. "I trust I won't be too much trouble for you."

"Not at all," said the grandmotherly Amica. "And who is this young woman?"

"This is Prisca," Servius said, stepping to the side. "She has come from Gaul, a refugee. Please treat her with care. She has had a difficult two days."

"I'll take good care of her, and see she is comfortable," said Amica, noticing the bruises on Prisca's face. "We will make sure she is healed well." She wrapped an arm about Prsica's shoulders, and gently urged her on. "Come, come," said Amica. "We will settle you in first." But Prisca looked back at Servius, who felt his heart tugged upon.

"It's alright," Servius said. "I'll be back soon."

As Amica and Prisca disappeared from sight, Titus and Servius went towards Orianus's home.

"Emperor Majorian is pressed today," Titus revealed. "With the Senate convening tomorrow, you will be sworn in by private ceremony today, after which time the general —I am sorry, the Emperor —will hold a private council with you and Senator Orianus." Titus adjusted his cape. "Do forgive me for speaking incorrectly. I served on the Emperor's staff when he was general."

"No apologies needed," Servius said as Orianus met them with his bodyguard, Claudius.

"I hope everything is, so far, to your satisfaction?" Orianus asked.

"I have not yet been inside, but I am positive that everything will be in order," Servius stated.

"I should indeed hope it," Orianus said with light laughter. "It was I who arranged your quarters for you, with the Emperor's approval. Shall we go and see him?"

Mounting horses, the two senators and their guards rode up the hill, through finely-tended gardens and carefully-kept cobbled roads, the houses and villas snuggled into the folds of the terrain. The Imperial Palace loomed ahead, fortified by innumerable soldiers in red and gold and yellow —members of the Emperor's Guard, Titus explained, more than a thousand in strength. They had been handpicked by Majorian from members of his old legion, and their loyalty was absolute.

Orianus and Servius were admitted at once, to a room with high ceilings, tall windows, and stone floors, with a promenade and commanding view of the city. There were several guards that stood about; a long, oak desk stood before the windows, its surface covered in a thousand papers and scrolls; and a set of doors, thrown open to the promenade, let in the midday light. Titus and Claudius remained outside while Orianus and Servius took seats at the table. No sooner had they relaxed, then the Emperor strode into the room, a host of military officers, a priest, and a senator trailing behind.

Orianus and Servius rose at once to Majorian, bowing, but Majorian waved off the formality. "You've journeyed too far for such trivial politesse," Majorian said, clasping Orianus's hand. "Welcome, old friend." The Emperor then turned to Servius. "And welcome to you. I trust the past few weeks since my visit have gone well?"

"For the most," said Servius.

"I heard about Colonia Paulus," Majorian said, shaking his head. "I won't stand for that kind of nonsense. Not while I rule Rome. Senator Orianus, you already know Senator Numerius. Senator Numerius, may I introduce to you Senator Servius, the son of the man who served in the Senate with you. Senator Numerius has long been, like Orianus, one of my closest friends and allies. Numerius is a native son of our city."

"It is a pleasure," said Numerius, a man of perhaps sixty. "I look forward with great anticipation to our work in the Senate, Servius."

"And this," said Majorian, gesturing to the priest behind him, "is Father Crispin, friend of the Pope, and my religious counsel and liaison to the Church. Father Crispin served in the field with us as well, in our war against Avitus."

The priest bowed his head reverently. "I thank God for your safe journey to Rome."

Majorian then turned to the officers behind him. "You men can leave. And the guards, as well. I am among friends, here."

Within a moment, the room had cleared, and Majorian had moved to the oak table, strewn with maps and information. He gestured for the others to join him.

"I have been emperor for a short while, since only December," Majorian explained. The civil war between us and the former emperor, the Visigothic-supported Avitus, has cost us dearly. As you recall, there was no emperor for that dangerous amount of time. The Senate has claimed much imperial power for itself while the selection of a new emperor was underway. I have been put into imperial power by the military, and by my own general, Ricimer, because there was no other choice. The legions are devoutly loyal to me, but there are not enough of them to defend our quickly-disappearing territory, as is evidenced by what has happened to Colonia Paulus."

"But it goes on," said Majorian, pulling forth a map of the Mediterranean and the Empire. "Beyond Rufus's Gothic confederation, all of Gaul is in rebellion; Spain has long been lost to us; northern Africa is no longer in our possession; the Vandals, the Goths, the Visigoths, the Burgundians, the rebellious peasant bacaude, and more peoples all seek to raise their hand against us while we are in disarray and unable to properly defend ourselves.

"Fiscal policy must be reformed, tax rates reformed, corruption in the Senate rooted out and the Senate and Imperial powers reformed. And I am confronted by social policy as well: abortions among our women are staggering, and the practice of keeping wealth stationary within families by forcing daughters to commit to religious celibacy, both mean fewer Romans being born to serve or defend, and the consolidation of power through money. Such vows also mean a plethora of sexual affairs between unmarried women and married men. Scandals are high and strife between Senators and aristocrats has never been greater. For them, Church only matters on political occasions. It is an obligation and a social duty for them, not an act of autonomous choice and commitment to Christ.

"Throw into the mix the Senate's divided opinion on my emperorship, grain shortages, a seriously-constrained treasury, and a number of senators moving to secure the throne for themselves, and we only begin to understand the size, scope, and plentitude of Rome's problems."

The three senators and the priest remained silent before Majorian, who sat down in a chair opposite them.

"Or," Majorian added, "my problems."

Just as quickly, Majorian rose again. "But, I am not without plans." At this, he threw aside one map, to reveal another beneath it, with bold red lines beyond the borders of the current empire.

"I fully intend to implement civil and fiscal reforms," he continued on. "But our most pressing concern at this moment is our frontier. The most immediate threat is Rufus. Rufus could topple us, if we let him. But if we fight him, he will not have the chance. Once Rufus is dealt with, I will begin to form an army, of Roman legions, auxiliaries, and barbarian mercenaries, and I will sweep across Gaul, and Spain, and Africa, retaking it for the Western Empire, and crushing any and all resistance. I will wipe away their militaries, and cement their subservience to Rome for the next century.

"But to do this, even to combat Rufus, we need troops. But troops are few and far between. So we will need to raise new legions. To do that, we must have funds from the Senate. But the Senate will not release funds without a majority vote. Because of the civil war, and other internal and external threats, the Roman Senate has usurped power to attempt to regain stability, and to make sure that an autocratic tyrant does not come to power and dispose of the Senate.

"With Ricimer and the military, I could easily cleanse the Senate, or altogether eliminate it. But that is not Rome. That is not our way. And our people deserve better than more internecine bloodshed. Besides, I somehow doubt God would tolerate any more such nonsense. So to regain my power as emperor, to raise new legions, to enact reform, I must do so legally through a legislative body that is, on the whole, opposed to all of it."

Majorian looked at Orianus, Servius, and Numerius.

"That is where we come in," explained Numerius. "I have already spoken with Senator Orianus last month, as I am sure he has already spoken with you, Senator Servius."

"He has," answered the young senator.

"Then you realize the urgency and the need for stealth. We are gathering an alliance of conservatives, republicans, moderates, pragmatists, Christians, pagans, patricians, imperialists, and anyone else who can be found who harbors many of the same beliefs. If a man is idealistic enough, then his convictions have already persuaded him; the pragmatists need something substantial to convince them, such as money or a deal. All of them have love for Rome in common, as well as a few, major concerns, such as organization for the defense of the Empire and the subjugation of the rebellion in Gaul."

"And that is where you are important, Servius," said Majorian. "You're an idealist, like your father. You can't be bought or sold or threatened. I knew his character, and based on the tax records you keep, as well as the words of Orianus, I know your character as well. When I visited you last month, I was uncertain as to whether or not I would appoint you to the Senate. I needed to meet you in person. And you convinced me that you would be a true friend and ally in this fight."

"And I will," said Servius.

"How many senators are with us?" Majorian asked Orianus.

"I have at least eight, all before arriving here. Tonight I meet with Senator Cleander."

"Senator Liberius's greatest ally," Majorian mused. "And Liberius is my arch opponent in the Senate. He is the wealthiest man in Rome, and one of the most powerful." Majorian folded his arms. "What do you hope to gain by meeting with Cleander?"

"Information," said Orianus. "To get a feel for what Liberius plans, what his intentions are this session. To see how many allies he has. And so on."

"You plan to retrieve all of that information from Cleander?" Majorian asked, amused.

"From both him and Liberius."

"We may be staunch opponents, as you know. But if there is one thing that neither Liberius nor his narcissist allies can resist, it is demonstrating their wealth and power and plans. Besides... a secret or two that are let slip won't matter with the kind of power and authority Liberius carries. The only cause of Liberius's doing will be Liberius. And he is not a fool."

Majorian nodded. "Keep me informed."

"I will," said Orianus. "I can be back here in the morning."

"Very well," said the Emperor. He turned to Servius. "Let's swear you in and make this official."

Father Crispin came forward, bearing a piece of cloth in his hands. "This is a part of the cloth worn by Peter, the rock and first Pope of Christ's Catholic Church," the priest explained. "Please place your hand upon it."

Servius did as was instructed, while Orianus, Numerius, and Majorian stood by as witnesses.

"Do you, Alban Servius, acknowledge that you are a citizen of Rome and a Christian of good faith?"

"I do."

"And do you, Alban Servius, accept the position of Senator as bestowed by the Emperor Majorian on this eighteenth day of March in the year of our lord 458?"

"I do."

"And do you, Alban Servius, swear by God and the Savior that you shall dutifully and loyally execute your office to the Christian faith, in service to Pope Leo, and in service to your Emperor, Majorian?"

"I do."

"Then as liaison to Pope Leo, and counsel to Emperor Majorian, I hereby confirm that you, Alban Servius, are a member in good standing in the Roman Imperial Senate. May God guide all that you do."

Father Crispin stepped back, and Majorian stepped forward.

"Now I can officially welcome you. I won't keep you or Senator Orianus but for a few more moments today. I'm sure you need to get settled in. You may come and see me any time.

"Tomorrow evening is the first of several imperial banquets, to celebrate the reconvening of the Senate. Yet we don't have time for those ridiculous formalities at the moment. I will dispense with ceremonies in the Senate, so that matters of the state can be discussed instead. I want the issue of Colonia Paulus front and center at once. The first thing we have to do is to make sure the Senate is aware of what has happened, as well as to underscore the human tragedy of it."

"A relief fund would be a good, bipartisan and unanimous way to begin," Orianus suggested. "That would be for tomorrow."

"And then, the day after, or in a few days as fit, we could elaborate on how this situation is being repeated all over the northern frontier," Servius added. "Thereby, the Senators could understand that the problem is not isolated."

"Good," Majorian nodded. "And then we the real work begins. We'll have to make the case for more legions."

"Is that a case that you could make?" Servius asked. "Or would it be seen as a challenge to the Senate's power?"

"Unfortunately," said Majorian. "I have to be seen as pursuing the law, not reinventing it. And that is why my involvement in our plan cannot be discerned. I must appear as detached from things, so as not to arouse fear or anger among the people or the patricians with the notion that I am raising an army for ends other than my own. Though my motives are pure and absolutist, I have to rely on the deft touches of a pragmatist in this instance."

"We shall embrace the fight," said Numerius. "I have grown up and grown old with this city. I will not let there be a repeat performance of what the Vandals did a decade ago."

Majorian nodded. "We'll save Rome, yet, not just from external threats, but from internal ones as well. Among the things I have done have been to temporarily transfer the seat of government back here from Ravenna. It is too close to the barbarians for my comfort."

Servius nodded. Half a century ago, the capital of the Empire had been changed from Rome to Ravenna, because many believed the other city's geographic location would be more suited to be defended, and would be in closer contact with the Eastern Empire. But there were many who were pressing for the return of

Rome to Rome. Among them was Majorian, who had shifted the seat of power back to the city.

The Emperor headed toward the door. "It was a pleasure to see you again," he said. "I'll see you in the morning."

Prisca had been given a room with two windows, one which overlooked the street, and one which overlooked the courtyard. She had been given clothes and sheets, and Servius had purchased a cross for her on the way back from meeting the Emperor. He promised to go with her and Amica to the markets, to secure for Prsica anything she would need following the Senate's first session the next day.

Her room was bare, for now, and was foreign and cold, no matter how warmly the lamplight glowed against the walls. She carefully set the cross Servius had purchased for her, as well as the cross her own father had created for her, on the nightstand beside her bed. She closed her eyes, and thought of home, of snowy fields, and her sister's laughter, and her mother's weaving. Tears fell down Prisca's face, and she went to the window for cool air.

It was then that she saw Servius. Servius had not eaten that evening, nervous and unknowing for what the morning would bring. He moved around the courtyard late into the night, from one bench to the next, around the pool at the center; he leaned against columns, bowed his head and prayed. For all he knew, hundreds of miles away, his own villa and his own fields might be burning, and every mountain town and northern village, a harvest of fire.

He was far away from home, too, Prisca thought; and it gave her comfort that she was not alone. She had been saved by the man who now paced circles around the courtyard, searching for something, searching for answers. Perhaps, she wondered as the torchlight glistened on the water of the pool, perhaps he had nightmares as well.

IV

As the sun rose in the sky, the darkness pulled back across the red-tiled roofs and gleaming marble columns of Rome, unveiling the streets and the markets, and beckoning the citizens, merchants, tradesmen, families, smiths, weavers, farmers, and peasants to their daily tasks and errands. But on this morning, criers announced the reconvening of the Senate, and a crowd of thousands turned out in the forum before the curia for a benediction from Pope Leo, to see Emperor Majorian, and to meet the new senators. From there, the people would go about their days, some optimistic, some less so; but a week's worth of celebration in terms of free games and entertainment at the Circus and the great Coliseum –at the Senate's expense –would put all in a better mood.

Servius met Orianus before his house along with their guards, and made their way to the curia by carriage. As they rode, their senatorial robes elicited cheers from young passersby, on their way with their families to the curia's forum.

"Just wait until we're passing legislation," Orianus quipped. "Then they'll be haranguing us."

"How was your meeting with Cleander and Liberius?" Servius inquired.

Orianus laughed. "They are as pompous and arrogant as ever, and just as dangerous. The make the veiled threat an art form. They revealed to me, in no uncertain terms, that they feel Rufus poses no real threat to Rome, and that we have too many standing legions as it is. They would prefer to hire foreign troops to defend us, and explained that anyone who calls for new legions to be raised will only be suspect in their eyes."

"That makes them suspect in my eyes," Servius acknowledged. "There is something not right, there."

"And that something not right is Liberius," said Orianus lightheartedly.

"I want to meet the man," Servius said humorlessly. "I don't understand how anyone could oppose defending Rome."

"You'll meet him soon enough," Orianus said. "And then you'll wish you hadn't. It is like plunging your hand into oil."

Vespius met Orianus and Servius as the foot of the steps to the curia, amid well-wishers, members of the Emperor's Guard, religious clergy, and fellow senators. The curia steps and the curia itself were bedecked with garlands and wreaths of flowers and laurels. The petals of roses, red, white, and pink, fluttered down from above like soft snow in the early winter.

Vespius was immediately about business. "I met with Senator Aurelius last night," he said. "I prevailed upon his wisdom and talents for land speculation and his family's inclinations for buying and selling. His family has suffered tremendously from the land lost in the

Gallic rebellion, but he is unwilling as of yet to commit to our cause. By my estimates, after speaking with Numerius, we have about twenty-five senators with us. It is by no means a sizable number, but it is not insignificant, either."

"And how many of them are truly with us?" Orianus asked as he returned the wave of a beautiful girl beyond the steps.

"Perhaps ten, including us. Ten out of one hundred active senators."

"So we have much work to do in the next two days," Orianus grumbled.

"Two days?" Vespius blinked.

"Including today," said Orianus. "The Emperor is just as urgent as we to move things along."

Above them, a band of trumpeters rang out their instruments, heralding the arrival of the Emperor.

"Up we go, to wait with the other Senators by the doors of the curia," Orianus said. "Welcome to public life, my young friend, Servius."

Escorted by a full cohort of the Emperor's Guard, with the lead ranks mounted on horseback, Emperor Majorian raised his hand from his chariot to the throngs, cheering wildly. Flower petals poured down from overhead, and maidens threw roses and lilies at the feet of the Emperor's horse team. As the column of guardsmen separated to stand opposite the crowd, Majorian ascended the steps of the curia, to be met by Pope Leo and Ricimer, the military commander of all armies. Both men bowed slightly to the Emperor, and Ricimer retreated to the sidelines as Pope Leo turned to the crowd.

"People of Rome," began the old pope. "May the blessings of God, and of our savior Jesus Christ, be with you all!"

At this, the crowd burst out into applause and cheers.

"I ask," continued Pope Leo, "that all Romans come together to pray for the guidance of our Emperor, our Senators, and our armed forces, so that the work of our empire can be done in the name of God. I ask for the eternal blessings and grace upon you and your families, and upon Rome."

The crowds cheered once more as the pope removed himself to the side of Majorian, who then came forward.

"Citizens and friends," he called over the masses, which fell silent to hear him. "On this day, with the blessings of Pope Leo, the Senate has reconvened to do your work. In the name of the Senate's honor, and at their expense, I announce a weeklong celebration consistent with the reconvening of the Senate!"

This brought the greatest and broadest cheers from the assembled people in the forum, something which perplexed Servius as he stood there, behind the Emperor. He knew that the people of the cities were known for their enjoyment of pastimes, but such an overwhelming response to the announcement of games reminded Servius of a drunkard begging for another cup.

As if sensing Servius's concern, or if reaching the same conclusion and expressing his own dismay, Orianus muttered under his breath, "They are animals."

"And now," Emperor Majorian went on, "I shall introduce you to the new members of this legislative body, so that you may see who serves you!"

One by one, the new senators —many of them ex-military, most of them in their thirties and forties — were called to the fore by the Emperor's side, and cheered by the people. Servius was summoned, and went forward to Majorian's side.

"I give to you Senator Alban Servius, of the northern Italian region of the city of Brixia. May God bless him and his service!"

The people cheered again their empty accolades.

"Enjoy it," said Majorian among the roar. "By tomorrow, half the city will hate you."

Servius raised his hand to wave, and the cheering continued.

Below, amidst the roiling masses of people, patrician and peasant alike, stood Marcellus, Amica, and Prisca. Prisca looked above, as Servius raised his hand, and the roar of the people around her was like deafening thunder. It was unlike anything she had ever experienced in her life; indeed, she never could have believed that such a city could hold so many people. She was comforted slightly by the presence of Amica and Marcellus, and was comforted to have seen Servius briefly on the steps beside the Emperor.

"You were blessed to have stumbled upon his villa," Amica said kindly. "He seems a good man."

Prisca nodded.

The curia doors shut and guarded by members of the Emperor's Guard, Majorian made his way through the main hall to the applause of the senators, taking the throne at their head. To the side sat Pope Leo, to observe and oversee the beginning of a new legislative session. Majorian remained standing, and the senators continued applauding until the Emperor raised his hands.

"Senators," he said. "Usually the first day of the return to the Senate is marked by ceremonies. But I ask that these ceremonies be postponed. I ask the Senate to discuss the matter of Colonia Paulus, one which will be brought to your attention by the noble Orianus."

With that, the Emperor took his seat, and Orianus rose from his place beside Servius and Vespius, to take center stage on the floor.

"Fellow Romans," he began, lifting his hands as if to implore. "I do not wish to postpone the ceremonies of the opening day of this Senate unjustly, but only to bring your attention to a matter of the gravest significance to all our hearts." He looked about the room, and Servius was surprised to see another man rise on the other side, one perhaps about fifty, and handsome.

"I, Senator Liberius," the man said, "do seek to hear the concerns of our noble fellow senator, and second the motion for the postponement of our formal ceremonies."

Vespius leaned over to whisper in Servius's ear. "Olive branch tactics are common early on," he explained. "Magnanimity sometimes impresses the heart where a purse of coins cannot."

"Then let us put it to a vote," said Emperor Majorian. "All those in favor of postponing initial formalities and ceremonies, announce it."

The response was unanimous.

"Let it be recorded," Majorian commanded the record keepers. "Senator Orianus, if you please."

"Men of the Senate," Orianus continued. "As you know, I inhabit the northern reaches of Italia, there residing with my old friend Vespius, and my friend and our new senator, Servius." At this, there was a murmuring of approval.

"The north is colder than your fairer climes here in Rome and to the south," Orianus said. "It is colder when barbarian activity rages on above us."

At this, Servius noticed the narrowing of Liberius's eyes, but his otherwise impassive face.

"My friends," Orianus explained, "I am not here to goad you into anything more than charity. The mountain community of Colonia Paulus has been put to the torch and torn asunder by Rufus's Goths. Good, honest, Christian, and tax-paying Roman citizens have been stripped of their lives, livelihoods, and homes. At this moment, the town of my residence, Colonia Caesarium, hosts innumerable refugees, from both Colonia Paulus, and refugees loyal to Rome from the Gallic rebellion. Senators Vespius, Servius, and myself have put together a temporary operation to feed, clothe, shelter, and find work for these refugees. But our resources are not innumerable. We are but humble farmers in the north."

"Humility and flattery," Vespius whispered to Servius, whom nodded in turn.

Liberius stood, and folded his arms. "Refugees, you say?"

Orianus nodded. "Indeed."

"Well," Liberius lamented. "We can't have them starve or go without shelter. What do you propose, noble Orianus?"

"A gesture of charity," said Orianus. "If we can prevail upon our aristocratic families to secure a fund to be administered by the Church, perhaps the Senate itself will also vote to match that collection?"

"An excellent thought," said Numerius, rising from his seat.

"I agree," said another senator, rising beside Liberius.

"Very well, Senator Cleander," Majorian said to the man. "Let us vote on the matter of securing a matching fund for those raised privately to be administered by the Church, to the relief of the refugees of the Gallic rebellion and the Gothic incursion."

The roll was taken; the vote was unanimous. As such, Liberius suggested adjournment of the Senate for the day, in order for the Senators to seek out private contributors. Majorian therefore adjourned the Senate to a thunderous applause, exiting the curia, followed by his guards.

The Senators then left their seats to converse and head out to the families of the Palatine. Orianus was congratulated on his benevolent act, and Liberius for supporting it. As Servius and Vespius watched the drift of senators throughout, Vespius smirked.

"Liberius has no idea, but he's just bought us the better part of this day to secure our allies. And here he comes now."

Liberius and Orianus, with Cleander behind, came before Servius and Vespius.

"Odd, isn't it?" Liberius beamed. "Normally we are in deep opposition. Amusing, actually."

Vespius deferentially bowed his head. "Better to be on the same side for such profound issues of Christian merit."

"Ah, yes," said Liberius. "Yes, indeed. And this must be Senator Servius. I am glad to meet you."

"And I, you," said Servius. "My father often spoke of your encounters."

"Your father was an honorable and intelligent man," Liberius opined. "Though we did not always agree, he and I always treated one another with the utmost respect."

"A tradition that shall continue," Servius said.

"An honor to continue it," Liberus replied. "I trust I shall see you at the banquet tonight? A few of my friends here in the Senate have arranged things to the last detail, from the quality of the girls serving the wine, to the quality of the wine itself. Fine wine without fine women is such a waste. But I'm sure I bore you."

"I will be in attendance," Servius said.

"Very good," said Liberius. "If only these banquets lasted year round."

"If they did," said Vespius, "we might well run out of women and wine."

Liberius laughed. "Never, never in Rome. I shall see you there tonight as well, I trust?"

"I would not miss it for all of Gaul," Vespius said with a smirk.

Liberius inclined his head. "Ah, yes. Gaul. Such a pity. I will see you this evening." Followed by Cleander, Liberius left the curia.

"His pomposity precedes him like stench before pigs," Vespius said, shaking his head.

Orianus laughed. "That bit about Gaul was quite amusing."

"I don't understand," Servius said.

"You see, part of the reason that Gaul rebelled, besides the fact that Avitus was dethroned and assassinated, was the levy of high taxes and the rejection of Gallic and Germanic officers in the imperial administration. Liberius opposed their expulsion, but favored raising taxes to keep the Galls in their place. He in part contributed to the rebellion because of it. But of course, no one blames him for the irrational actions of barbarians. That, and he has enough wealth and power to make up for his mistakes. Women adore him, senators want his power, boys want to grow up to be him… And it disgusts me."

"And now, what?" Vespius asked.

Orianus thought a moment. "We'll meet with Numerius, and begin going to see different senators. Individual visits. If a senator seems persuadable, but remains undecided, we'll all go and see them."

"Where shall we meet?" Servius asked.

"You're not going," Orianus replied quickly.

"What?" Servius said in disbelief.

"You're not going with us to visit senators," Orianus stated.

"I thought I was a part of this enterprise? Shouldn't I be allowed to speak with them?"

"Oh, you will be, but not right now." Orianus took Servius's shoulder in a fatherly manner. "Look… You're a newcomer to this Senate. There are a handful of other newcomers, all of them loyal to Majorian because they are ex-military. You are the only civilian recruited by the Emperor to the Senate. That puts you in a unique position."

"For what?"

Orianus lowered his voice. "To be the one to push for new legions."

"I don't quite follow," Vespius said, his mind attempting to surround the thought.

"If one of Majorian's ex-officers calls for new legions, Liberius will use it to say that the Emperor wants more power. The military backs Majorian. The Senate does not wholly do that. How would it look if ex-officers called for more legions to be put at their former commander's disposal? I'll tell you: like an overthrow. Liberius would be unstoppable then, gaining supporters left and right. Yet if our friend here, Servius, who has farmed and is a newcomer to politics, and is the northernmost living senator, calls for troops to defend the central northern regions, then the image of a power play by the Emperor becomes untenable. We would force Liberius to either support or oppose the measure."

Vespius nodded, and then turned to Servius with a smile. "Do enjoy your afternoon."

Servius, Prisca, Amica, and Titus went through the markets below the Palatine Hill a short time later. The warm sun swept broad light across the paved streets; the population of Rome bustled about the arrival of fresh produce from the farms beyond the city walls, and the smell of baked bread drifting among the smells of vanilla, lilac, and roses. There was laughter, and there were forward-looking faces all around. Wherever Servius went, he was bowed to and greeted kindly.

With Amicus's assistance —and while Servius and Titus waited outside —Prisca found new clothing, seeking few sheer, thin items, and favoring a more moderate linen appropriate to her station. Amicus explained that often the senators preferred younger females in their employ to wear such translucent items, but Servius said that such clothing was not necessary. The servants could dress as they pleased. Servius also made sure to find a beautiful, sky blue silk ribbon upon which Prisca could fashion her cross.

Servius also made sure that sheets, blankets, and other personal amenities needed by Prisca were secured, as well as a new shawl for Amicus for her troubles. While Prisca secured the more feminine things with Amica, Servius went to the next shop over, full of scrolls, books, codexes, and various pamphlets and papers. He moved among the shelves, from philosophy, to theology, and finally, to a section with Christian writings. There, he found the works of Ignatius of Antioch, and John of Damascus, and Jerome of Stridonium, including the one anthology he was seeking. Wrapped up in soft cloth, Servius kept it under his arm on the ride back to his house.

Titus's shift ended, and he headed toward the port to see if his family had yet come in; and Titus's replacement, a soldier named Horatio, came to stand watch at the house. Horatio was a veteran of the wars against the Huns, and of the recent civil war. In his fifties, Horatio said little, but commanded enormous respect from his fellow soldiers, including Titus, who assured Servius of the loyalty of Horatio to Majorian.

Prisca was settling into her room once more, putting away her new robes, when a knock came at the door. She was surprised to see Servius, and she bowed.

"Please," said Servius. "That isn't necessary."

She rose and took a step back, but would not look him in the eyes.

"Are you comfortable, here?" he asked, though plainly could see she was not.

"I am adjusting," she said softly.

"Is there anything else I can do?" he wondered.

"No, but thank you."

"Well, I hope I haven't interrupted you. But I have something for you I picked up today." He placed the linen-wrapped package on her table.

"What is it?" she asked.

"Find out." He smiled.

But rather than reach for the package immediately, she looked up at him. "Thank you," she whispered. "For everything."

"You'll always have a home with me," Servius said. He then gestured toward the package, which Prisca approached carefully, gently pulling back the cotton linen. Her eyes lit up, and they found Servius's.

"The Vulgate," she whispered.

"One of the most authoritative Bibles there are," Servius affirmed. "They're still working on a standard canon of texts, but so far, Jerome's Vulgate seems to be the best."

"Thank you," Prisca said, clutching the book against her chest, tears brimming at her eyes. She sat down on her bed, and began sobbing; and Servius suddenly wondered if he'd done something wrong.

"What is it?" he asked, kneeling before her.

"This book," she said; "My mother read to me from the Vulgate every night when I was little. To have a copy of this... So wonderful..."

"You're welcome," said Servius. "I thought it was important that you had a Bible."

Prisca looked up at him, biting back her tears, and reached out to touch his cheek. "Thank you."

He took her hand in his. "You're welcome."

Gently, she opened the cover, to find an inscription there to her, from Servius, thanking God that she had come to his household. When she looked up to him again, he had already disappeared from the room.

V

When Liberius had told Orianus that every detail of that evening's banquet had been planned to the last detail, Orianus knew he meant it. Arriving at the imperial household in dress robes with Servius, the walkway to the great hall where the banquet was to be held was lined by slaves from the interior of Africa, from Gaul, and from the Levant, wielding torches; arrayed beyond them by the entrance were members of the Emperor's Guard, watching carefully all those who came and went. The path to the doors had been salted with rose petals; the doors themselves were attended by lightly-clad slave girls, who took the outer robes of those who were arriving. Servius, however, kept his robe to himself, explaining to Orianus that he was far too formal to remove it except in his home.

Inside, curtains of sheer linens in crimson, gold, and white, descended from the ceiling above; chairs and couches littered the room, covered in throws of burgundy and deep violet. Senators and aristocrats sat and stood about, drinking wine, laughing, admiring one another, and the slave girls that attended them.

"Normally," Orianus said, "these banquets are for two reasons: to drink and to go to bed with as many women as you can get your hands on, anywhere you can. Past the drink, Emperor Majorian has forbidden such sexual acts at his banquets, because beyond his Christian faith, he believes such outlandish behavior under his roof only ensures bad blood between politicians and citizens. The real party will be afterwards, at Liberius's villa. This, you could say, is simply a formal gathering compared to what is to come."

Servius shook his head. "You're talking about an orgy."

"That's exactly what it is," said Orianus. "They occur, day after day, night after night in this city. Welcome to Rome." With that, Orianus took a cup of wine from a passing slave girl, and took a drink.

"I'm not sure I shall attend one of those," Servius said, breathing in deeply.

"It will be a social obligation," said Orianus. "You learn to live with them. Putting in an appearance is expected if you are invited, but participation is not expected –though choosing not to is looked down upon."

"Even by Christians?"

"Most of us are Christian," said Orianus. He gestured toward where Liberius sat among three girls, one of them a slave, the other two aristocrats. "Or at least, most of us pretend to be."

"Orianus! Servius! How are you!"

Both men turned to find Vespius approach, his arm around a female aristocrat. Orianus smiled and shook his head.

"I can see you've already found company for the evening."

"Of course!" laughed Vespius. "What was I supposed to do? Wait around for you two?"

"Certainly not," replied Orianus. "We'll be perfectly content seeking out women of our own."

"Ah, yes," said Vespius. "Oh, and I ran into Liberius earlier. Almost knocked him over, too."

Orianus laughed and Servius looked toward where Liberius had stationed himself, surrounded by women, and the rich and the powerful. Noticing the three of them, Liberius waved them over.

"Oh dear God," Vespius said as the woman to his side kissed his neck, "into the lion's den we go."

As they approached, Liberius rose to meet them. "Orianus, Servius, Vespius! It is good you're here." Servius noticed that among Liberius were also positioned Cleander and Capito. Capito's close association with Liberius struck Servius as disconcerting.

"You know," Liberius went on, "when you spoke of Colonia Paulus today, I sincerely thought you were going to call for one of our frontier legions to head up into the mountains. I almost laughed."

"Purely an eleemosynary effort," Orianus said, dismissing Liberius's thought.

"Please, please," Liberius said. "Do sit down."

At his invitation, the trio of senators took places around Liberius. "So what do you think?" he asked them, gesturing about the room.

"Magnificent," said Vespius, holding the aristocratic woman against him.

"Of course," said Liberius, "it would be much better if our Emperor would allow some of our traditions to continue unchecked, but oh well. When the guests come to my villa from here, there will be no shortage of traditions." At this, he caressed the cheek of one of the girls, who sat at his feet. As Servius watched this action, he suddenly thought of Prisca, and the possibility that she might have ended up in such a place, with such a role. But he shook the thought from his mind.

"We look forward to later," Vespius grinned. "So very much."

Servius suddenly had the desire to leave, to be rid of the party, to be back at his house further down the hill, or even to be back in the Senate. He seemed to be among strangers rather than senators. But no, he realized, it didn't matter. Rome mattered. It had to.

"And how are you finding Rome thus far?" Liberius asked Servius.

Servius made himself nod. "Very well, thank you. It is a marvelous and unique place."

"I am glad you find it so," Liberius said. He leaned forward to take another cup of wine from a passing slave, and stood. "Forgive me, but I am off to make my rounds. You have to be everywhere at these things... Lovelies?"

At his beckon, the three girls with Liberius rose to follow him across the room. Cleander quickly made an excuse that he had an introduction to make, and stalked off to be with his political allies. That left Servius, Orianus, and Vespius with Capito. Capito smiled.

"And what do you have to say, Senator?" Vespius inquired as he dismissed the woman at his side.

Capito leaned forward, and lowered his voice. "My cousin, Senator Laurentius, as well as Senator Longinus, who owns several southern gladiator schools, are both in."

"And what is the price Longinus commands?" Orianus queried.

"That you indirectly purchase slaves from him to help form one of the cohorts in the first legion that is formed."

"Gladiators are not cheap," said Vespius. "The Senate would never allow such a thing."

"I'm not talking about a contract," Capito said.

"Then what? Private funds?"

"No, no, no," said Capito, with an air of omniscience. "He will donate the gladiator slaves —two hundred of them —in exchange for the dismissal of the tax arrears case against him."

"Ah," said Orianus. "All he has to do is purchase two hundred miscreants and call them gladiators."

"I cannot comment on the quality of the slaves he will donate to our cause. But I can say that he will be in our corner, you will have at least two hundred men to fill the ranks, and it will not cost the treasury a single coin. All for a measly case dismissal, too."

"We will do our best," Vespius said.

"I'll let Senator Longinus know to begin selecting slaves," Capito revealed as he stood to head across the room.

"That will fly directly against the tax reform policies the Emperor hopes to implement," Servius said boldly.

"That is true," said Vespius, impressed by the young senator's ethics. "So we shall simply ask the Emperor to wait on his tax reforms until after the

Gothic crisis is abated, and then carry forward his desires for reform."

Servius said nothing.

"Pragmatism," Orianus said kindly. "Pragmatism doesn't always come at the expense of loyalty or beliefs. Sometimes, it is simply a matter of timing."

"I understand that," said Servius; "But what if we are short on time?"

Vespius said nothing, then; and Orianus steeped his head in thought.

"I suppose," Servius said in answer to his own question, "that principle and pragmatism must compel priority."

"Well stated," Vespius affirmed. "And that is a principle for which I shall always stand."

"You should all stand," said Senator Numerious as he approached the three. "The Emperor wishes a word with you. But do not leave directly. One at a time, leave the room, so no one else notices your absence together."

"Understood," said Orianus. "I believe I could use some more wine."

"And I believe I just saw a pretty young thing wander past," said Vespius, standing.

"And you, Senator Servius," said Numerius, "may entreat yourself to a tour of the garden. I'll show you there."

"I should be interested to see the gardens," Servius said as he stood to follow Numerius.

When Servius and Numerius appeared in the gardens, the emperor was discussing something of great importance, for Ricimer, and other military officers had gathered around him. Father Crispin sat patiently on a stone bench, listening to things.

Majorian noticed the approach of both Servius and Numerius. "Good," he said. "We have much to talk about." Vespius, and then Orianus appeared behind Servius and Numerius a moment later.

"The situation is worse," the emperor said quickly. "I've just been informed that four more mountain villages have been razed."

"These aren't just raids," Ricimer growled, spitting on the ground.

"Forgive Ricimer," Majorian said. "He may not be a Roman, and may be of barbarian origin, but you will be hard pressed to find a Roman more committed to our cause than he."

"Proof of Rome's civilizing effects," Vespius said haughtily. Ricimer glared at him.

"Regardless, Ricimer is correct," Majorian went on. "These aren't just raids. Rufus is testing our defenses, seeing how far he can push us, seeing what kind of mettle we have to offer in return. We still haven't heard from the transalpine cohort; they may have been massacred for all we know, or perhaps they simply put down their arms and went home. Rufus is not an idiot. The other thing he's doing is testing and mapping out routes through the mountains.

"We also know that a late snowstorm has swept northern Italy, making the mountain passes unfit for travel. We may have a few days, or a week, perhaps more, so long as the cold weather there keeps the snow from melting, before Rufus is back in force. He must know by now there is nothing standing in his way.

"Orianus, you are one of my closest friends in the Senate, as are Numerius and Vespius, here. The snow may be a saving grace for the people in the northern reaches, but not for us, here. We're out of time."

"Then we must have troops," Servius stated matter-of-factly. He breathed in slowly, surely, aware of what needed to be done. "I will make a call for troops in the Senate tomorrow."

"And I will second it," said Vespius without hesitation.

"You're sure you're willing to do this, Servius?" Majorian pressed. "Liberius and his allies will come down on you like fire."

"Better them than the Goths," said Servius. "I could not call myself a Senator if I was unwilling to risk this position for the people."

Majorian nodded, wordlessly, approvingly. "I will give you the evening to think this through," he said. "Because if you are committed, you must stay the course. You cannot falter once you have made this call, no matter how difficult things may become. They will lambast you, seek to humiliate you, call into question your faith, your integrity, your character, your motives. Think it through. And if you are committed, be prepared for the host of questions, insults, and charges Liberius and his minions will fire off at you."

"Then I will stand as I must," said Servius.

"You will not stand alone," said Orianus. Vespius and Numerius nodded in agreement.

"Still," said Majorian. "Take the evening. If, tomorrow, you intend to go through with it, then bring it up on the floor." The emperor frowned. "If Roman men applied conquest to the battlefield the way they did women, fame, and fortune, then Rome could not fall," said Majorian regretfully. "Many of the people in this city take seriously their Christian belief. But there are many more, like Liberius, who give alms with one hand, while reaching for power with the other. That is what Liberius truly wants: power. Yet he does not care at what expense. Service is a foreign term to him. Servius, just be prepared for what you will come up against. That is why I want you to think on this well."

"Then I will do so," said Servius.

"What do you know of Servius?" Liberius asked Orianus as the guests began to arrive at the second banquet. Cleander turned toward Orianus to see what he had to say. Orianus furrowed his brow; he had been expecting the interrogation, sooner or later.

"That he was a farmer, that he is honest, and that he is very traditional," Orianus tactfully revealed.

"A conservative," laughed Liberius. "How quaint. But no, tell me more. You've lived within miles of him his entire life. We all knew his father. But what about the son?"

"Until Emperor Majorian appointed him to the Senate, I had little contact with him," Orianus replied. "He is something new to all of us."

"Oh, Orianus," said Liberius with mock exaggeration. "You bore me. You know more than you let on. But I suppose, considering he is from the northern extremes, he should be in league with you, and the Emperor, God bless him."

"Ah, Liberius," remarked Orianus. "You yourself are a native to the north."

"By birth only," was the quick reply. "No, no... My destiny, my life has been in Rome."

"So what is it," Orianus said, returning the subject, "that you find so interesting about Alban Servius?"

"As I had mentioned, his father was in league with you. I'm sure the son already is. I'm also curious about the fact that he is the only senator appointed by Emperor Majorian who does not have military service under his belt. And as you know, admiration for the military, or service in our armed forces is not the glorious thing it used to be."

"Thanks in part to you, Liberius."

"I eschew military service. It is a waste of time for anyone, and Roman citizens are better off letting others handle the dirtier aspects of life." Liberius paused a moment to return the wave to three girls —obviously from below Palatine based on their clothing, obviously uninvited —who passed through the door without effort. "I do enjoy those sorts of guests," he rambled. "Ah, yes... But to return to your friend, Servius. Do not think for one single second that I am an idiot, or that I am unaware something is going on. We may be fellow Senators, and we may be opponents on nearly every issue, but that doesn't mean we have to be enemies." Liberius turned to Orianus, and lowered his voice. "Don't make me your enemy."

Orianus smiled. "Then don't make Rome yours."

Liberius rolled his eyes and cleared his throat. "Cleander, what do *you* think of Servius?"

"I think he is an idealist," Cleander voiced coldly. "Idealists are easily beaten down when confronted with the harsh reality of politics."

"Either that," said Liberius, "or they prove impossible to stamp out. Do you know what I think?"

"What is that?"

"Senator Servius strikes me as somewhat unconfident, but dangerously capable of what he sets out to do. He already is in the good graces of the Emperor, and he appears to be able to make friends quickly." With that, Liberius smirked toward Orianus. "But let us also remember that it may be just as easy for him to make enemies."

Prisca had not expected Servius to return as early as he had. Illuminated by flickering torchlight, Servius went around the courtyard as he had the previous night, arms behind his back, his mind obviously unsettled; his heart, too, perhaps. It was both a comforting feeling to see him back, but also disconcerting to see him ill at ease —comforting, because Amica had explained what a royal banquet was like to her, and she hoped that Servius would have no part in such things, though why, she was unsure; and disconcerting because she was unsure if there was anything she could do.

She sat down on the edge of her bed, but rose again to look through her window to the courtyard. She looked at her father's cross on the silk ribbon Servius had purchased for her, as well as the cross and Bible he had purchased for her as well. She blinked back tears, thinking of home, and her family, now gone; and she thought of Amica's kindness, and how, at the very least, she had a place to be.

No matter how much she hurt, she knew that she had to earn her keep, to make sure Servius was not wasting his time and money on her. Silently, she slipped from her room, and headed to the kitchen, where she pulled from the shelves a small cup, filled it with water from the pottery that contained it, and carried it out to the courtyard.

Servius, his arms folded, turned his gaze from the pool to Prisca. The light from the torches touched her eyes, like starlight in the night sky; and the cool, calm breeze that drifted through the courtyard tousled her hair about her shoulders.

"I thought this might help," she said placing the cup on the nearest stone bench. She bowed deferentially, and retreated to her room immediately.

And then he remembered how to breathe.
She was a welcome interruption from the thoughts at hand. He went to the cup she had set down, and took a sip of the cold water.
Tomorrow, he would make the call for troops. He would support the emperor. It might be the end of his senatorial career —after two days —but it didn't matter in comparison to the greater cause. He was a farmer, and could return to his farm. Like Cincinnatus, though Cincinnatus turned down inestimable power and wealth. Servius would turn down nothing. He had nothing to lose, and nothing to gain. He would return to the farm, one way or another, in victory, or in defeat.

Victory. Victory was the only option. New legions, Servius thought, would require a commander to be victorious. Majorian could not lead the troops, not while Liberius held so much sway, and not before Majorian consolidated his power. Ricimer would not be a popular choice with most senators of any political persuasion, and besides, Servius thought, there was something untrustworthy about the man. Flavius Aetius was dead. So there was one man who could do it, Servius thought. A Roman citizen by birth, who had spent his life in the military. One which Servius's own father had spoken highly of, but little was said about the man since he had served under Aetius against Attila and the Huns.

Tremissis Scipio, Aetitus's most competent commander. That was who could lead the new legions. A man who knew war. A man who could lead. A military man that Majorian could trust. Such a man who had defeated the Huns could be trusted by the Senate as well —and trusted by the people to shatter Rufus's designs on Italy.

Scipio it would be.

VI

"All hail the Emperor Majorian!"

"Hail, Caesar!" came the reply from the Senators as the emperor made his way to the throne on the floor. Servius sat between Vespius and Orianus. His heart was quick and his chest heavy; he felt cold, and his hands shook just slightly from time to time. He had not spoken in public before, except to small groups of people on mundane issues, such as local taxation and parochial celebrations. This was something entirely new.

"I open the floor to all matters of business," Majorian declared.

"The formalities of the first day of the Senate," Cleander said, taking the floor, "would be a good place to begin."

Majorian leaned forward. "As Emperor, I herewith dismiss the formalities for this session."

Servius put his hands on his knees, and breathed in deeply. Majorian was helping to clear the way.

"Emperor," said Liberius then, standing. "I wish to report on our collection for the victims of the raid at Colonia Paulus."

"Very well," said. "And then I have pressing news on that front."

"I shall be but a moment," said Liberius in deference. "Between the imperial banquet and my own, we have raised eight thousand denarii. I ask the Emperor and the Senate if we shall meet and match that contribution?"

Affirmative calls rang out through the curia. The Emperor stood.

"We shall now vote," he declared. "All those favoring matching the relief fund, to my right; those opposed, to the left."

The senators stood; not one remained opposite the right.

"Then let it be done," said Majorian to the record keeper, and the senators resumed their seats.

"And now," said Emperor Majorian, himself taking the floor. "I bring to your attention a matter of the utmost importance. Beyond Colonia Paulus, four more Roman villages in the Alps have been raided." At this, a murmur spread throughout the curia. "That makes five villages that have been attacked by Rufus."

Servius looked across the room at Liberius. As the day before, Liberius scowled, clearly anticipating something.

"Senators," Majorian explained, "I bring these sad facts before you to make you aware of the difficult situation of our northern citizens. I cannot tell you what to do in this instance. It is up for the people's representatives to determine the best response. I therefore open the floor to discussion."

As Servius expected, it was Liberius who rose first.

"Fellow Senators," he called. "It is a tragedy what has happened to these villages. But with all due respect to our beloved Emperor, who himself can only give to us the information his commanders give to him, how do we know that Rufus is responsible for these attacks?"

Servius rose slowly. "I can answer that if the Senate-"

"Senator Servius," said Liberius, smiling and shaking his head. "We welcome you among our number, and look forward with great eagerness to your contributions, but perhaps in this instance, someone of greater experience can speak to this issue."

"That is exactly what I was proposing," said Servius. "I ask the Emperor's permission to bring into this curia a guest, one who waits just beyond the doors, who can speak with the authority of the church and of the village to the just question that Liberius poses."

Liberius clenched his jaw as he looked towards Majorian, who turned to one of his guards.

"Go and bring in Servius's guest."

Servius and Liberius remained standing as Father Marcellus was politely ushered into the curia. Marcellus made his way toward the emperor, bowed slightly, and then turned to await the word of Servius.

"This is Father Marcellus," said Servius. "He was the priest in Colonia Paulus. He can speak where I cannot. I yield to his expertise." With that, Servius sat, and Orianus patted his shoulder.

"It is an honor to address this body," said Marcellus, reflexively touching his bandaged head. "You ask for an account of the razing of my town. I shall give it."

Marcellus made his way to the center of the floor.

"The Gallic rebellion had sent many refugees through our town as of late. Loyal, Roman citizens and taxpayers, fleeing before the Gallic civil war, and the raids of Rufus's Gothic confederation. As you know, Rufus is gathering various barbarian tribes to his banner, having gone from a single band of rogues to a powerful, ranging force. There have been no shortage of reports from those passing through our town to confirm this, including among them, fellow priests.

"The farmers of Colonia Paulus, who had gone out to test the fields last week, to see if they could be turned, reported seeing black-clad riders in the valley below us, and on the mountains above us. These sightings were reported to me, and so I set out one morning with them to see for myself. Sure enough, these riders appeared again in the distance. I at once sent word to the transalpine cohort, and they responded that they would be sending a patrol up to ascertain who these riders were. Yet, they never got the chance.

"Three days ago, as you know, our humble town was burned, and the church sacked. It was a small mountain town of a few hundred people. A large number of them are now dead and buried in the snow. The Goths struck us at first light. They pulled me from the church, and the last thing I remembered was a spear shaft swung at my face. When I awoke, the village was burning, and two of the townspeople had taken me onto a wagon. From there, we made way to Colonia Caesarium."

"And that," said Orianus, to reinforce the point, "is when I sent word here to the Emperor, and to the surrounding regions and towns."

"And what would you have us do?" Liberius asked, his words slithering away from his tongue like venom. "Pull our legions from the west and the east to traipsing through the snow after a band of horse thieves?"

"They were not horse thieves, Senator," Marcellus said ruefully.

"With all due respect, Father Marcellus," Liberius drawled. "I did not deign compare an enemy of Rome to a horse thief. Rufus is not a threat to Rome." At this, there was a wave of murmuring throughout, but Liberius was undeterred. "Rufus and his hacks are taking advantage of the Gallic rebellion and divisions within the Goths to strengthen his own position. He is not after Rome. He is after his own ends. He pokes at us, to demonstrate his strength to his followers and his enemies, but he will never confront us head on." There was some cheering.

"It doesn't matter what his motives are," said Numerius, rising from his seat. "What matters is that he has attacked Italian villages, that he has attacked Roman citizens, and therefore, he has attacked Rome herself." Many senators voiced their approval to Numerius. Majorian leaned back in his seat.

Liberius shook his head. "Friends and worthy adversaries... We cannot fault anyone in this room who has the interests of our Empire at heart. Yet, they overreact. Going after Rufus —which is what the noble Liberius seems to suggest —would be like swinging a hammer at a fly. It would do more harm than good."

Just as Servius was preparing to rise, Cleander stood.

"I have a thought on the matter," Cleander said. "Perhaps we should wait for word from the transalpine cohort to carry on this discussion any further. My good Emperor, you say you have already sent men out to ascertain this?"

"I have," replied Majorian.

"And dear Orianus," said Cleander. "You will as well have sent men to the fort where the cohort is stationed?"

"I did indeed," replied Orianus.

"And this was three days ago?"

"It was."

"Then the earliest we should hear back, could possibly tomorrow."

"Depending on the rider, the horse, and the winds for the sea," Orianus confirmed.

"Then why not wait to see what they have to say before we decide to take action?"

"An excellent thought!" Liberius declared amid the vast approval of the legislature. "Let us make an informed choice!"

Servius looked over toward the Emperor, who but his bottom lip, but kept his outward demeanor otherwise calm. He rose, glancing around the room, making care to linger on Servius just a moment, to make sure Servius understood that the call for legions could not come today, and then continued his gaze around the curia.

"Then we shall await word from the cohort," the Emperor announced. "We now move on to the issue of nonpayment of taxes in arrears."

"That foul idiot!" Vespius said as he stood before the house of Servius, along with Orianus, Marcellus, and Numerius. "Five villages, and Liberius is not convinced that this is more than just a Gothic show of bravado."

"In times past," Servius said, reflecting on the histories that lined his shelves, "we would not have even stood for one raid."

Orianus folded his arms. "It speaks volumes about the times about the living when they must worship the dead."

Servius did not attend the second imperial banquet. Rather, he remained at home, in the study of his house on Palatine Hill, having collected about him the works of Julius Caesar's campaigns in Gaul. When Caesar fought, Rome was stretching her legs, expanding her borders, taking allies by diplomacy, and conquering by force. When Caesar fought, Rome was often outnumbered, but more times than not, successful. The same was true of Augustus, and the successive emperors. Even in more recent times, such as when Aetius fought Attila at Catalaunian Plains, Aetius had only auxiliaries and barbarians at his disposal —yet nevertheless won the day. And so Servius carefully studied the battle, noting geography and quick action to seize the high ground resulted in the repulse of a Hunnish assault, which then began the descent to disaster for Attila.

He read in the courtyard, under the open sky. As the night came on, the torches were lit, and he sat on one of the benches, contemplative, reflective; the firelight shimmered in the water.

Prisca, who had been through the market for most of the day with Amica, picking up foodstuffs and household supplies, was preparing a late dinner with her.

"The others tell me he's been studying those books for hours," Amica said, gesturing toward the courtyard. "They told me he's been reading up on our city's military history."

Prisca breathed in heavily. "Do you think it will come to more war?"

"I do, unfortunately," said Amica. "And it is not something that I welcome, for my son is in the IV Legion. And you, Prisca, have already lost far too much."

Prisca nodded solemnly. "At some point," she whispered, "we do have to stand and fight."

Amica wrapped her arms around her young charge. "You're a wonderful young woman," she said. "Any many would be happy to have you. You should go and bring the senator something to drink. I would imagine he hasn't had anything at all today."

"I will," said Prisca as Amica returned to her preparation of carrots.

As she had the previous evening, Prisca gathered some water in a cup, but also took out to Servius a freshly-baked roll. She approached quietly, not wanting to disturb him; and as she crossed the courtyard toward him, he looked up at her –and her heartbeat quickened. She suddenly felt comfortable.

"Thank you for the water yesterday evening," he said, their eyes meeting. "I would have thanked you this morning, but I had to attend a meeting with Orianus and Vespius."

"You're welcome," Prisca said. "I spent most of the day at the markets. Perhaps you could tell me the things you most like to eat, and that way, I could prepare them for you." Without waiting for an answer, Prisca set down the water, and handed the roll to Servius. "Amica didn't think you had eaten anything at all, today. And I think she's right. You should eat. Dinner will be a little longer."

"Thank you for this, too," said Servius. "I'm sure, though, that whatever you prepare, I'll enjoy."

Prisca gave him a polite smile, and went on.

As Servius took a bite from the roll, Titus stepped into the courtyard.

"Sir," he said. "The Emperor is here."

Servius stood at once, and followed Titus to the front gate, where Majorian, accompanied by a host of guards, dismounted his horse.

"Don't bow," said Majorian as he approached. "I could not handle it from a friend. I thank you for your discretion in the curia. But that is not why I am here. We received word moments ago from Orianus's messengers. The entire transalpine cohort has been undone, and their fort burned to the ground. There are only a few survivors. It was Rufus, it was the Goths, and they appeared before the fort numbering more than a thousand. That isn't a raiding party. That is an expeditionary force, with the target being our only major military outpost in the central mountains. More than seven hundred dead Goths littered the ground, along with several banners bearing Rufus's symbol of a skull and arrow. They probably figured they lost too many men to keep the fort, so they burned it. If Rufus can afford to send a thousand men against a fort, he must have thousands more.

"You are the first to know about this," Majorian divulged. "I have sent word to Orianus, Numerius, and Vespius as well."

"Then I will confront Liberius and the Senate with this information," said Servius.

Majorian nodded. "That was a stroke of brilliance, bringing in that priest. It certainly impressed upon everyone the seriousness of the situation. I have the messenger, Gladius, that you may call upon tomorrow, if you wish it."

"I will," said Servius. "I'm sure you already know by now I'm committed."

"I do," said Majorian. "And I swear to you before God that, one way or another, I will protect you for your bravery. Gladius has carried with him one of the banners, a plate of chest armor, and a sword from one of the dead Goths. It should make quite a show in the morning."

"Very well then," said Servius as Majorian returned to his horse.

"And Servius," said the emperor as he prepared to ride back to the palace. "God keep you safe."

"There has been a supported motion by Numerius that we return to the issue of the northern raids," Majorian announced the following morning in the curia. "And so we will."

Liberius, as expected, stood. "Noble friends and worthy adversaries," he said from his place. "Did we not, a mere twenty-four hours ago, rule that we should wait for such evidence as is substantive to demonstrate the reality of the raids?"

Servius stood, taking a deep breath. "We did indeed, honorable Liberius."

Liberius smirked. "So then what are we doing speaking about this again?"

"You seek proof," Servius affirmed. "And that is what I have to offer. Emperor, if you would permit one of your guards to bring in Gladius, the messenger sent by Orianus three days ago."

The smirk quickly disappeared from Liberius's face as Majorian bade one of his men to bring in Gladius. Orianus could not resist smiling himself as Gladius arrived, carrying a small wooden crate, which he set down on the floor.

"Your name is Gladius," Liberius said as the senators strained to catch a better look at the box.

"It is," the messenger replied. "I am a member of Colonia Caesarium's militia. I served at Catalaunian Fields against the Huns as an auxiliary."

"And Orianus sent you to Colonia Paulus?"

"No," said Gladius. "I went to the transalpine garrison's fort, to see if they were aware of the raids."

"And were they?" Liberius said.

"They were," said Gladius. "Most of them were dead."

Liberius, for the first time, said nothing. The senators began talking amongst themselves excitedly, but Gladius continued, and the senators quieted down.

"I went on Senator Orianus's instructions to alert the transalpine cohort, to have them send troops to Colonia Paulus. But when I arrived, the fort had burned, and there were a handful of survivors. The fort had been besieged by more than a thousand Goths for two days. They finally carried the fort by storm. The survivors were members of an observation post higher up on the mountain that were trapped, but saw the battle. There are hundreds of dead Gothic warriors that cover the ground around the fort. Their surviving elements withdrew, but for what reasons, I'm not sure. Perhaps because they had lost too many men to keep the fort themselves."

Liberius found his voice again. "And how do you know they were members of Rufus's Gothic confederation? How do we know they weren't simply rogues? Or more to the point, considering the Gallic rebellion, how do we know they weren't Gallic troops?"

"Because the attackers wore the armor and carried the weapons of Goths. And because the attackers held these, which bear the symbol of Rufus's confederacy." Gladius removed the lid from the crate, and held up the black banner that bore the skull and arrows. Now there was an uproar in the curia, and Liberius's face had gone red. Vespius couldn't resist laughing.

After a moment, Liberius raised his hands to quiet the room down again.

"Very well," he said, lowering his voice as silence returned to the curia amid the faces of anxious senators. "I say that we adjourn for the day" –and he was forced to raise his voice again against the voices of others –"I say that we adjourn for the day so that the senators can see the evidence for themselves, and can take the day to consider it."

There were calls of affirmation, and rejection. The emperor put it to a vote, and those favoring adjournment outnumbered those who opposed it by eight.

"Very well," said Majorian. "We adjourn for the day."

At once, the noise returned to the curia, as the senators began speaking to one another, some raising their voices, some speaking hushed, concerned tones. Orianus, Numerius, and Vespius at once went about, singling out senators that had voted for adjournment. Majorian and his guards left, while other senators circled about Gladius, asking more questions about the massacred cohort.

"I'm not sure what you think you're up to," said Liberius in a dangerous, condescending tone as he came to stand beside Servius. "But do be aware that no one – no one¬ –humiliates me, in public or in private, especially some backwoods upstart three-day senator whose path to a seat in this body is solely because his father's lifeless body was there for him to step upon."

Servius breathed in deeply, and his hands formed fists at his side.

"Consider this your warning," Liberius whispered angrily. "Do not test me again."

"I would suffer your wrath for Rome," Servius said. "I would suffer a thousand deaths against men like you."

"Do not... test me... again..." Liberius repeated, making sure to enunciate each syllable. He then stepped away, and left he curia through a herd of his supporters.

That night, Orianus, Numerius, and Vespius dined at Servius's house, in the courtyard. Vespius was still laughing, as he had been in the curia.

"The look on Liberius's snub face," he howled, wiping away tears from his eyes. "I've never seen him in such a state of humility!"

Orianus smirked. "It was a powerful, powerful performance, one which we owe to our friend Servius, and the Emperor."

"Oh, that there were a way to see it all over again!" Vespius guffawed.

"You did well," said Numerius. "Your timing was exceptional."

Orianus leaned forward. "As humorous as Liberius's overreaching was," he said, bringing gravity back to the conversation, "Liberius is not a man to be taken lightly. We all know who he is and what he can do. He will not suffer today for long. And Servius will, unfortunately, be his target."

"I will not let him stand alone," said Vespius, patting Servius's back. "We're in this together."

Prisca, watching from the kitchen, was at various times, felt both proud of Servius for whatever he'd managed to accomplish in the Senate —but also unnerving fear at the warnings Orianus offered. Whatever was happening, she realized, was of monumental importance.

"I propose," said Senator Liberius the following morning, "that our first order of business will be the demise of the transalpine cohort, and the burning of the five northern villages." The proposal was quickly carried.

"Rome is an irresistible, undeniable, unconquerable force of nature. It is like the rain. It cannot be stopped. It will cover the world like a flood once more, and with it will come the light of civilization and knowledge," Liberius began. "Yet the question is how such a thing shall occur. And the circumstances that lead us to discussion are tragically noted, but enlightening in their formation." At this, Liberius glanced at Servius.

"Our garrisons north of Italy only invite trouble!" Liberius orated. "That does not speak to the cohort so recently done in, for it was within our territory, but it does speak to the garrisons north of Italy. They are targets for our enemies. Yet, the solution to the problems of our extraterritorial garrisons and the security of our citizens rests within the very problem itself. Why are the Goths, the Galls, the Visigoths, the Alans, the Vandals, etcetera, etcetera, poised against us?" Liberius looked around the room.

"They want power. They want what we have. And there's no reason we shouldn't let them have some of it. There is no reason to have Roman troops beyond our borders! Roman law is good enough to preserve the peace –and so is pay."

The senators stirred as Liberius stepped in a great circle on the floor. "Why should we fight the barbarians when we can pay them to do our bidding? We've paid barbarians before, made and broken alliances with them. Rather than risk Roman troops, we simply pay others to do the same work."

"That is nonsense!" said Numerius, standing from his seat. "If the Goths wanted to be a part of this empire, there is no reason to raise arms against it!" There was affirmation and dissent throughout the curia.

"A Roman citizen can bear a sword and shield; so, too, can a paid mercenary," said Liberius.

"A Roman citizen and a barbarian are not one in the same," said Servius, standing. Liberius turned his gaze to the younger senator as he descended to the floor. Liberius narrowed his eyes.

"Numerius makes a good point," Servius expounded, feeling the heat rising in his face, feeling the eyes of the Senate upon him. "It is one thing when a barbarian seeks to become a Roman, to learn our ways, to live as we do. But it is something else entirely when they attack us and kill our citizens."

"The loss of our citizens is regrettable," said Liberius, turning his attention solely to Servius, who himself realized he was being marked as an enemy. "Yet we must distinguish between reason and madness. No more Roman citizens should have to die to protect our northern frontier, if we can pay Rufus to do it for us."

"That is traitorous to our people!" someone in the room shouted amid the cries of others. Liberius remained calm, however.

"What would you propose, Senator Servius?" Servius took a deep breath. "Raising a new legion of troops."

The curia returned to an uproar.

"Why," shouted Liberius, "should we raise a new legion? We have no need for a new legion!" The room began to settle, and Liberius resumed a normal voice. "Have you all forgotten the civil war we recently emerged from? Have you all forgotten the tyranny that too large a military can exert? The creation of such power will invariably lead to corruption."

Majorian leaned forward in his seat. "I trust that my position is not corruption," he said icily.
Liberius turned without a shred of composure lost. "You are an exception to the errors of the armed forces, Emperor" Liberius said. "You're the reason why we have order and why the military remains loyal to the people." At this, the Senate broke into applause for Majorian.

"What do you propose?" Majorian asked Liberius directly.

"Why, a simple olive branch," Liberius intoned. "We send a diplomatic mission to win over Rufus. Once he is on the dole, then he will not cut off the hand that feeds him."

"And what if he does?" Vespius said, rising and coming to stand by Servius's side.

"Then a new legion can be discussed," said Liberius without hesitation.

"I propose," said Orianus, taking the floor beside Servius, "that we can compromise here. If we are to fight Rufus, we will need more troops. At the moment, pulling our legions from the frontiers is dangerous. So let us raise a new legion at the same time Senator Liberius sends out his diplomatic overture. If the overture succeeds, we simply disband the legion, or reinforce the existing legions by distributing those men recruited. If the overture fails, Rome will have a solid protective force against Rufus."

The room broke out in applause all around, and Majorian looked impressed. The color had drained from Liberius's face, but he quickly recovered.

"How will you raise a new legion to combat Rufus in the next week or two?" Liberius wondered aloud.

"We will call up reserves, reach out to veterans, bring together auxiliaries, and take in new volunteers. The veterans and the reserves will form the core of the unit, and will help with the training of volunteers on the march. When it comes time for battle, the volunteers can be used as guards for the camp, or for reserves on the field. The veterans, the reserves, and the auxiliaries would otherwise be sufficient."

Liberius looked amused. "And who would you propose to lead this remarkable little legion of yours?"

Servius breathed in deeply, and spoke loudly.
"Tremissis Scipio."

The room at once exploded in laughter. Servius was unprepared for the response. Orianus and Vespius were not laughing; a handful of senators remained motionless.

"Dear boy," laughed Liberius. "Your heart is in the right place but your mind is absent. Tremissis Scipio is a washed out drunk, who has spent more time in bars and brothels than on the battlefield. It's bad enough you've managed to cobble together even some modicum of support for an unneeded defense force, for my diplomatic overtures will succeed —but to seek to engage Tremissis Scipio to command an army? You might as well lead it yourself!"

There was more laughter, but Liberius's face took on a look of manipulative delight, and bemused malfeasance. "Yes, yes, that is what we shall do. You shall be in command of the army, and then you may hire Scipio at your judgment! This entire venture will be on your shoulders! And when my diplomatic plans succeed, you alone shall be held accountable!" There was more laughter, but there was booing against Liberius as well. Majorian shifted in his seat, his gaze deadly; Orianus and Vespius continued to stand beside Servius.

"Then I shall command the army!" shouted Servius, above the roar.

Liberius reached up his arms to bring the curia to order. He took another round of the floor as he spoke again. "Oh, you may command. But I wonder, if, besides our new senator's apparent knack for organizing a legion, if he has any idea of the cost of doing such a thing. Thousands of denarii to raise and properly equip the men, and thousands more for rations and other materials. That means contracts from the Senate, through the imperial treasury. You'll need a majority in the Senate for any of it, and you clearly do not have a majority."

"Then such a legion can be privately funded," said Numerious.

"Nonsense!" cried Liberius. "Treason! No man may privately raise an army!"

"Numerius is on to something," Servius said. "I had anticipated concern over funding, and the Senate would be justly concerned about its expenditures."

"Did not just hear what I said? No many may privately raise an army! It is against Roman law!"

"No man may raise an army," Servius said. "But certainly men may fund an army that will be overseen, ultimately, by the Senate and Emperor of Rome."

The roar of competing opinions was deafening, and now Servius raised his hands to quiet the room. "Think about it, honorable senators," said Servius. "A defense force, paid for by the people, overseen by you. I will take full responsibility for it. The Senate shall bear no cost in terms of risk, but will certainly be able to reap the reward of the people's gratitude. Let the noble Senator Liberius send out his diplomatic mission, and let the defense legion be put together!"

Majorian rose from his seat and took the floor, from which the present senators retreated out of respect.

"If the Senate should be so inclined as to hear my opinion, I should like to give it."

Servius, watching Majorian from the side, knew full well the Emperor could silence the Senate to give his opinion whenever and wherever he wanted, but for reasons of tact, he was taking a more respectful approach. The Senate acceded to Majorian.

"I believe that both Liberius and Servius present important points of view, and important responses to the crisis at hand. I believe that a dual response, one predicated upon and initialized by diplomatic outreach, to be followed up by a military response if appropriate, is the correct method to address the crisis. There is nothing in Roman law which forbids a publicly-funded legion, overseen by the Senate and the Emperor. I believe we should bring this to a vote as a solidified plan."

Liberius raised his hand, and was acknowledged by Majorian.

"I, too, believe we should bring it to a vote," said Liberius. "But I also believe that we include the caveats that Servius indeed take full responsibility for the defense force, and if it is deemed unnecessary, that he will reimburse the public by paying for free games at the Coliseum for as many people as can fill the stadium once a day for two weeks."

"I accept that amendment," Servius announced.

"And," added Liberius. "Another caveat, if so disposed… While Servius may have overall command of the legion, with the ultimate control belonging to us, he will need a military commander —either that drunken fool Scipio, or someone else to serve with him. A senator, without military experience, is simply unacceptable."

"I accept that amendment as well," Servius declared loudly.

"And Liberius… Will you personally take responsibility for the diplomatic mission to Rufus?" Majorian posited.

"I will," said Liberius. "But," he added quickly, "I am not a diplomat. Someone with such experience might be better suited."

"Then who will lead the diplomatic mission?"

"I will," said Numerius, emerging from the crowd of elected representatives. "I have commanded many such missions before. And I would be honored to bring the force of Rome for peace once more."

"Do you accept this, Liberius?"

Liberius nodded.

"Very well then," said Majorian. "Let the Senate now vote on the matter at hand. Affirmative, to the right; rejection to the left."

The senators rose, some talking to one another, some idling for a moment before leaving their stations, and they begin to trickle down across the floor. One by one, every senator came to stand on Majorian's right.

"Servius, you may raise your defense legion. Numerius, you may organize your diplomatic mission with Liberius."

VII

The afternoon was busy. Orianus organized his house to receive peasants and patricians alike in order to donate to the defense legion. The Emperor officially approved the mobilization of the reserves, put out a call to younger veterans, and sent word to local auxiliaries to come to Rome. At last, a volunteer call was put out to the masses.

Servius watched from the front of his villa, with Prisca and Titus beside him, the stream of Roman citizens who had heard about the call for funds, and had responded. A long line of people curved around their road, and back down the hill. "It is unlike anything I have ever seen," said Titus. "And you'll notice that most of them are humble farmers and tradesmen, donating a Cistercian or two as they can. I'm even amused to see a priest or two in line to donate as well."

"News travels fast among the people," said Servius. "Of the raids, the cohort, and the call for help. Tomorrow, the legion begins organizing outside the city, along the Cassian Way. Vespius has taken on the task of securing lodgings, while Capito and his cousin are bringing up arms from their city stores. Senator Longinus, because of his gladiator schools, has the staff needed to feed the troops, at least for the short term. And that leaves me to enlist Scipio."

"Tremissis Scipio?" Titus asked.

"The same."

"Forgive me, sir, but Scipio? His days of honor have passed."

"There is no other choice," said Servius. "I thought long and hard about it for the past two days. Who else is there?"

Titus did not have an answer, but did have a question.

"You're to command this army," he said. "I wish the honor of going along as well, to continue in my service to you. I am positive the Emperor will allow me to do so. Will you?"

"If that is your wish," said Servius, "I am happy to have you."

"And I am honored to be here."

Majorian stood outside the curia, surrounded by guards and senators, including Liberius, Numerius, and Cleander. A few hundred people had gathered around them in the late afternoon sunlight, in the cool spring breeze, to watch the diplomatic escort make its way out of Rome. Numerius would be the sole civil servant, along with a few aides, a translator, and an escort of fifty cavalrymen from the Emperor's Guard.

"Do recall," said Liberius, as Numerius stepped into a carriage, "that your actions will dictate how all of this plays out. Failure is not an option."

Numerius looked out at Liberius gravely. "If I fail, it will be because I have been killed." With that, he tapped on the side of the carriage, and the escort went forward, leaving Majorian and the others to watch it disappear through the streets.

Servius, Titus, and Horatio rode their horses through one of the poorer sections of the city. As they went along, most people waved happily at the senator, aware of what he was doing on their behalf. The others looked upon Servius as a rich elitist who had no business in their part of the world, just as they assumed they had no business in his part of the world.

"The last time I saw the general," said Horatio, speaking of Scipio, "it was in one of these taverns." Servius looked around, disappointed but not surprised in the great number of pubs and brothels in the area, though it perplexed him: another section of the city he had ridden through a few days before, arguably just as poor, had no such places of ill-repute, but had churches instead.

"There are dozens of such places in this neighborhood," said Titus. "We're going to have to go through them, one at a time, until we find him."

No sooner had Titus said this, then a commotion kicked up two blocks ahead. A short, stout woman chased a late middle-aged man into the street, waving a broom about her. They could only hear bits of what she said, but as they approached, her words were clear.

"And don't come back until you can pay me for your drink, you rotten swine!" With that, she returned to her place of business.

"That," said Titus, pointing toward the obviously drunk man parading up the street, "is Tremissis Scipio."

Servius looked at the man stumbling down the street, eliciting laughter from a few passersby, and worried whether or not he might be in over his head. But he was already in, and he urged his horse on.

"General Scipio!" Servius called out. The man did not respond, so Servius called out again, "General Scipio! A moment, please!"

At this, the old general turned around, his face full of stubble and his hair unkempt; his clothes were bedraggled and filthy, and he was wearing only one sandal.

"What do you want?" he spat as the three men approached. "I've paid my taxes. Go back to the Senate and you know what you can tell them to do with themselves."

"This isn't about taxes," Servius said, dismounting. Titus dismounted as well, while Horatio held the horses.

"Then what are you stopping me for, boy?" Scipio said. "I've a very busy schedule, and a date with a woman or two tonight." Without waiting for an answer, he went on, and Servius caught up with him, and began walking beside him.

"I am Senator Servius. I'm here to ask you a personal favor, on behalf of the Senate."

"There's nothing personal about that miserable body of legislators," said Scipio. "They're a waste!"

"I don't entirely disagree," said Servius, keeping pace with Scipio, who surprisingly kept up a brisk walk.

"Then what on earth are you doing in the Senate?"

"I was appointed by the Emperor."

"How well and good, the gods or God be praised, whoever you on the Palatine are praying to these days."

"General Scipio," said Servius, a touch of anger present in his voice. "I pray to God and I'm asking for one moment of your time. That's all."

"Right," said Scipio, turning to face Servius. "Go ahead."

"You're familiar with Rufus's Goths?"

"Yes," said Scipio. "Everyone and their mothers are talking about it. Well you know what I say? Let them raid this cursed city. Let them raze it to the ground."

"I am putting together an emergency defense force, a temporary legion, if you will. It is being raised to defend the central northern passes of the Alps against Rufus. I have been appointed to command, but I'm a farmer, not a commander. I want you to be the military commander of the legion."

Scipio's face contorted in confusion. "You want me to what?"

"Lead the legion against Rufus," said Servius.

Scipio burst out laughing. "My God," he said. "After Aetius is murdered by Emperor Valentinian, the Senate strips me of my command and my estates, my wife divorces me, and now the Senate wants me back? Ha!"

"There is no one else to do it," said Servius quickly. "At least no one else I can rely on. At least not with your experience."

"The Senate is always cooking up something half-witted. Count me out of this! I'm too busy!"

"General Scipio," Servius said forcefully. "If you don't do this, no one else will. And Rufus will come through the mountains, burning and pillaging, hitting our frontier legions from behind, and they will march on the city, and you will have nothing left here."

"No," replied Scipio. "I think your moment is up."

"The time has not yet come," said Servius. "For myself, or for Rome."

"Spoken like a philosopher," Scipio laughed. "There are better options to command your miserable legion."

"My father spoke very highly of you," said Servius.

"I knew him," said Scipio in a moment of clarity. "One of the few truly noble noblemen."

"It is on his word alone that I would seek you out for this job, your service under Aetius notwithstanding."

"I'm touched," Scipio spat. "Find yourself another lackey. The wars are over for me. The Rome you want to defend doesn't exist anymore." He began to walk away.

"You once pledged your life for this Empire," Servius called after him. "You swore an oath, and you defended it honorably. You have to do this again for the people, for all of us. For yourself!"

But Scipio did not answer, and merely continued on down the street. Titus came up to stand beside Servius. Servius felt as if he had failed, as if the ground had given way beneath him. *The Rome you want to defend doesn't exist anymore.*

"Let him go, sir. We can try to find someone else. And besides, we have to go. Vespius will be expecting you at his banquet."

Servius remained on the front steps of Vespius's city estate, and was warmly congratulated by senators and aristocrats, businessmen and patricians, generals and priests as they passed by, on his performance in the senate; yet Servius felt cold. *The Rome you want to defend doesn't exist anymore.*

Servius had heard Orianus and Vespius speaking with Capito. The arms were secured and already paid for; there was enough funding to equip one full legion and provide it with rations for a month, and even the Church had donated to the pool. Word had spread quickly among the people about the dual plan for handling Rufus, and the city was, unexpectedly, not panicked. For the time being, people spoke positively, openly, about the Senate, and Majorian's already strong popularity as emperor had only grown exponentially.

But there was not Scipio. And there was not Rome, either... And suddenly, Servius's own faith in Rome seemed somehow diminished. Inside the house, in Christian Rome, a pagan celebration; the right cause, the wrong means. *The Rome you want to defend doesn't exist anymore.* The city at night was alive with such wrong means.

"Senator Servius."

Two girls, teenagers, clearly aristocrats, appeared before him.

"We would be honored to keep you company this evening," said one of them.

"Very, very much," said the other. "We'll be inside. Please don't forget us."

Servius nodded politely, and the two of them went through the door; out came Orianus.

"I was wondering if you'd join us at all," said Orianus.

"How can that happen?" Servius asked, gesturing towards the two girls.

"They find you powerful and attractive, I'm sure."

"Not that," Servius brooded.

"The feasts, the banquets, the behavior of Romans," Orianus acknowledged.

Servius shook his head in the affirmative.

"The Rome you saw that morning we came into the port was mostly a façade. It was a veneer of normalcy, against the great upheaval of flesh and sin and the rot eating us alive. There are good people, but there are not enough, at least here, in the city. The people indulge because it keeps them happy, and helps the Senate keep them in line. The Church condemns such indulgent behavior, and Majorian will not allow it in his residences. Some would say the city is better than it was before Constantine; others would say it is worse. Either way, it is unacceptable in its present form. And I heard about what happened with Scipio."

Servius breathed in the chilly air. "Do you know what he told me? He told me that the Rome I'm fighting for no longer exists. So what is it that I'm doing?" he wondered aloud.

"That," said Orianus, "is something only you can answer."

"I'm committed," said Servius, a revelation unfolding. "But I don't know what I'm doing… or why." He looked at Orianus. "I'm going to go. I need to think about all of this. Alone."

"I understand," said Orianus.

Servius stepped down from the house, and into the street. Horatio appeared a moment later, but Orianus held out a hand to slow him.

"Give the senator some space. Make sure he gets home alright, but give him the space to be alone right now."

"I will, sir," said Horatio.

Servius walked alone that evening, down the quiet streets of a residential quarter, most of the occupants a few blocks over, attending late shows, performances, or in the brothels and the privately-hosted orgies, pursuing conquests of the evening, of sex and skin, drink and hot flesh. Rome was a roiling sea of some kind of sin, leaving few places untouched. Across the street ahead of him went two girls, unclothed, from the door of one house, and into the door of another. Even here, there was no respite. There was no place in Rome to be alone.

He stopped, in the middle of the street, a cool wind across his neck, and a cold air against his heart, ice in his veins. All at once he wished it would be destroyed, all of Rome, every single brick overturned as it had been for Carthage, and the ground salted; the prostitutes would be rooted out, the corruption exposed and the corrupt forsaken, and the rest of the Empire to replace the City, with the Republic restored, virtue returned, the foundation once more secured.

How easy, though, he mused, to fall into the embrace of some girl, a thousand of them, night after night, to enjoy the wine and the wealth and the fame for being Roman, without actually understanding what it meant to be Roman. No, he was not surprised that such things proved to be so seductive, so compelling, so easy to do for so many, for most –at least in the city. For beyond the city, the farmers still tended their crops and raised their families. Rome was a city, an Empire, a place far away and out of sight, heard but not seen, spoken of but not experienced, dreamt of once upon a time, but never truly realized.

Dear God, he thought. Dear God, how could it be so? Saving the Empire would be mean preserving the decadent lifestyles of the rich and the poor, the gluttonous, the heretics, the whore, the adulterer, the drunkard, the atheist, the sexual deviant, the prodigal son, the fallen daughter, the corruption of politicians, the Liberiuses of the world. But all for what? To what end?

Yet, all at once, the question was answered for him in his own mind, in his own heart. Preserving the Empire meant preserving the possibility of a better tomorrow. Saving Rome meant saving the Church, the family, the farm, the industrious, the virtuous, philosophy, politics, law, technology, medicine, the arts, architecture, the flame in the night.

"Senator Servius."

He turned. Prisca stood there, before him, wrapped up in his cloak.

Saving Rome meant saving angels.

"I followed you. I'm sorry. I waited up for you, and I saw you come by the house, and I saw you stop, and look up, and continue on. And I wondered where you went this evening, and so I followed you. I… I was worried about you."

Servius smiled. "I'm sorry to have caused you such concern. I was thinking."

The torchlight cast beautiful, glowing patterns across her face, and her eyes were alive with the radiance of light. She approached him, closing the distance between both of them, and she looked up at him, the fear still prevalent, still new, afraid that he might somehow disappear inside the night.

And Servius felt his heart tighten, his breath quicken; the ice and the cold were gone, and so was the darkness.

"I suppose we should head back," he said at last.

Prisca, without a word, linked her arm in his —a bold thing to do, she knew, but she needed to hold onto him, hold onto something sure, and she felt him unsure and uncertain at first, but then he pulled her against him gently, but determinedly. She knew he needed it, too.

"I'm not sure I know where we are," he confessed.

"I do," she replied.

"Do you?"

"I've been here all along."

"Forgive me for not seeing," he replied softly.

She stopped him, and reached up, and touched his face, ran her soft fingers over his lips, felt his breath on her fingertips, and she pressed his hand to her mouth.

"I meant it when I told you that you owed me nothing," he said.

"This is not an obligation," she explained. "And it won't be just for tonight."

"Then let it not be tonight," said Servius, kissing her forehead, summoning up every shred of moral courage he contained. He could feel her heartbeat racing against his chest. "Let it be in its proper time, and its proper place."

She knew he was speaking of marriage, that he took his Christian faith seriously, just as she took hers.

But whereas, in this instance, she had been willing to compromise herself to keep him somehow, he had refused to betray his conscience. And it was a profound moment of understanding, understanding who he was, and that he truly was worth holding onto. She would live her life serving him if it meant being near him for another day. And perhaps, she thought, perhaps he would marry her. But then as suddenly as the idea flooded her heart, the gates were thrown open. She was nothing. And he was a Senator of the most powerful Empire in the world.

"You're a good man," she said softly, her voice carried on with the wind.

"And you have a good heart," Servius said in return. "And you should always follow it, no matter what."

He went on, and she held onto him as they went back. His mind raced, and his heart seemed torn apart, by hope and despair, by day and by night, by faith and by sin, by love and by regret. He had a duty to Rome, right or wrong though Rome was. And now there was this girl, this beautiful girl that had somehow found her way into his life. He had always intended to marry, but there was never the right time or the right place. Based on the past week, he knew Prisca could make a wonderful wife, the kind of wife that every Roman male citizen dreamt of, but few ever found. He had been lost, somehow, without ever realizing it, and she had found him.

Before he went to sleep that night, they stood in the courtyard, and he kissed her fingertips before he turned in.

Prisca took the kisses on her fingertips, and rested them against her heart when she laid down that night. They were soothing, and kind, and calming, and her fear of being alone had left her entirely. Perhaps, she thought, perhaps there was a chance after all.

When Servius awoke the following morning, his resolve had fully returned. He had stayed up later, praying to God, thinking to himself, wondering what could be done. And then he thought of Prisca, of the family farms, of everything that would be wiped away if no one stood to defend it. He entered the courtyard, to find Marcellus, Titus, Horatio, Orianus, Vespius, and Capito present. Servius smiled at Prisca, who emerged from the kitchen.

"We were concerned," Vespius began, but Servius put up his hand kindly.

"I will lead the legion, even without Scipio," Servius announced.

"No need," Titus said, stepping into the courtyard. "He's here."

VIII

Much sobered, though still looking as if he'd had a rough night, Scipio appeared before the group of senators in his military uniform and armor, itself worn and faded. His sword was present at his side, and he held his helmet under his left arm, and raised his right.

"Good morning, Senator Servius," he said. He bowed his head to the others present. "Senators."

"I'm glad you could join us," Servius said. "How did you know where I lived, though?"

"I followed the people leaving flowers at your doorstep. Does the offer to command the defense force still stand?"

"It does."

"If I am to command," said Scipio, "there will be conditions."

"I understand. Name them."

"While you may have overall command, and I support that, I will make the military decisions. I will have absolute command on the battlefield, should it come to that. And if I should present you with an order while on the field, I expect you to obey it. And I will receive the pay of a general, not a legion commander."

"I can accept that," Servius stated. "But I also have conditions."

"State them."

"No drinking until after the crisis is handled. We will conduct ourselves as Christians, and will observe ethics and the just war criteria put forth by Augustine."

"The drinking I can manage," Scipio said honestly. "Just war... I'm not entirely sure what that is. But I suppose I'll have you to keep me informed."

"If it comes to it, yes."

"Then I accept, if you will have it."

Servius nodded. "I do."

"Shall we go to the Cassian Way?" Orianus suggested.

"Yes," Scipio agreed. "Let us see what I am to command."

With Scipio and Servius in the lead, followed by Titus and Horatio, Vespius, Orianus, Capito, and their guards in tow, the group set out for the fields that fell along the Cassian Way. As they wound their way through the city, the people moving around noticed the company of senators and soldiers, and few flowers were laid in the path of their horses. But the simple acts of honor did not impress Scipio.

"So now that you've had a good taste of Rome, why is it you still want to fight for the whore that she is?" the grizzled general asked.

"It took me a while last night to understand that myself. But I figured it out. It is because Rome is an idea," Servius said. "Because there is still something of

Rome worth fighting for. It is more than this city. It has always been more than this city."

"You really do believe that, don't you?" Scipio turned toward his younger comrade.

"I do," said Servius. "With all of my heart." He paused, and looked at Scipio. "And what changed your mind?"

"I needed a job to pay for my drinking."

Vespius laughed behind them.

"Well," said Servius, "at least you're here."

"I'm not a priest," Scipio said. "I can't call down God from Heaven."

"But you can make a legion march and fight. And that will do."

Outside the city walls, the morning sunlight warmed the earth, and the quiet farmhouses stood out bright against the land. The trees, yellow-green with early spring, stood atop the hills and nestled in the hollows of the countryside; wildflowers in pastel blues and gentle purple appeared throughout the meadows as the stars appeared on the night horizon. Less than a mile outside Rome lay Aurelian Field, site of an old fort, and a place where Roman citizens came to celebrate festivals and rendezvous with secret love.

But Aurelian Field on this day had transformed into a makeshift military encampment, one which stunned both Servius, and Scipio. Before them were thousands of men, some in uniform, some in civilian clothing, some adorned in purchased armor and holding purchased weapons; and thousands of civilians – daughters, sons, wives, mothers, fathers, sisters, grandparents and fathers –moving among the camp with baskets of food and jugs of water. Some tents had been thrown up, some rudimentary wooden shelters had been erected, and elsewhere, canopies stood to shade the people beneath them.

"This is the Rome I fight for," said Servius breathlessly.

As Servius and his group approached, they were recognized by the people before them, and a thunderous cheer went up at their approach.

Scipio looked at Orianus, and then at Servius.

"Raise your arm, Senator Servius," said Scipio. "This is your doing. And that's my first order."

Servius raised high his right hand and waved, and the crowd continued cheering.

"The first thing we need," Scipio said realistically as the cheering continued, "is order. This may have sprung up naturally among those who responded to the call, but we have got to get this into form. Disordered, undisciplined men are more a danger to themselves than the enemy."

By noon, a command tent had been set up, and the weapons had come to the camp. Scipio had set to work at once seeking two more military officers to serve as his adjutants, and to help him put the camp in working condition. Modius, a veteran of the wars against the Huns, and against the Goths, and a current member of the reserve army, was given the task of compiling a list of those present for duty, and to respectfully dismiss those unfit for service. Modius, an old friend of Scipio's beyond his military experience, was also appointed the task of finding capable commanders to lead each cohort, and each century therein. Titinius, a very old veteran but very capable veteran of the Civil War of 394, was given the task of quartermaster by organizing the camp's logistics, appointing details for kitchens and cooking, latrines, rations, supplies, and weapons inspections. A skilled physician and medical assistants were secured as well.

Servius went among the camp, followed by Titus and by Horatio, seeing the progress that had transformed a massive sea of faces into something that did indeed resemble the order of a regular legion's activities. It was at noon that Scipio and Servius met with Orianus at the command tent, to hear the reports of both Modius and Titinius. Yet it was Modius's report that interested the commanders most of all.

"This is what I've come up with," said Modius, reading from a muster sheet. "We have two cohorts worth of reserve troops released to us, at the strength of 1,200 men; 3 cohorts, auxiliary troops, 1,800 men; one cohort of able-bodied veterans, 300 men; one cohort of gladiators from Longinus, 200 men in strength; and a cohort of fit civilian volunteers, including farmers, tradesmen, metalworkers, field hands, civil service workers, and athletes, among them an entire archery team that performs regularly at the Circus Maximus. Altogether, we have 3,900 men available for combat duty. As support to various details in noncombat roles, we have an additional one hundred men. Taken together, that's 4,000 men."

"I am surprised we have that many," said Scipio. "But no active duty troops."

"No, sir."

"That will cost us," said Scipio. "Have you selected competent commanders for each of the structural divisions?"

"I have, sir," said Modius. "And we're already commencing training with the civilians, and gladiators. The gladiators have single combat skills, but they need to learn discipline to work in tandem with an entire unit. The civilians need just about everything."

"That is good work," said Scipio as some cheering went up among the camp. "What on earth is going on now?" he said angrily. "This is supposed to be a military camp."

As Servius, Scipio, and Orianus stepped out from beneath the command tent, Emperor Majorian reared up his horse before them.

"Good morning, men!" he called. "I hope you'll have room for a few more additions to your ranks?" With that, he pointed down the road behind his aides, at a column of soldiers, the lead ranks mounted, the succeeding ranks on foot –Emperor's Guards. "I am releasing a cohort of six hundred of them for your command," Majorian explained. He turned to his left. "This is Quintus Decinius. He is a loyal friend and an invaluable soldier. He will serve you in just such a fashion as the commander of the cohort of Guards."

"We're happy to have them," said Servius.

"And happy to have active duty, combat experienced troops," Scipio said.

"I'm glad to see you decided to participate, old friend," Majorian acknowledged gratefully.

"When last we met, you were under my command. Now I am under yours."

Majorian saluted his old general. "You'll forgive me, but I have pressing matters to return to. Servius, if there is anything you need, you know where to find me. I'll see you in the curia."

Servius bowed his head, and the emperor and his group rode off, heading back to the city, and the cheering continued. It was loud enough to be heard on the city walls, from which curious city reserves and citizens looked out over the land.

Standing alone and aside, Liberius and Cleander watched the emperor and his aides riding back toward Rome, and heard the distant ovation dissipating.

"We have a serious dilemma," Liberius said icily.

"I don't think anyone could have foreseen this," Cleander offered. "I swore the trouble would come from one of the new, ex-military senators, and certainly not from some low middle-class farmer."

"Servius is our most major threat," Liberius conceded. "We will never be able to reach a compromise with Rufus if he continues to act out, or if Servius is allowed to challenge Rufus on the field. The diplomatic outreach under Numerius will succeed, however."

"Will it?"

"I sent a code in the message to be delivered to Rufus, hidden in plain sight. I told him to withdraw from the Alps, and to bide his time by going after the Galls or the Alans instead."

"And you're certain Rufus will accept this?"

"He had better," Liberius said, placing his hands on the wall. "He had better indeed if he expects to rule Europe without Roman opposition."

"Then we had better remove Servius," Cleander commented. "I'll send word to my spies to see what they can find."

"It would be a waste of time with him," Liberius gritted his teeth. "I doubt you'll find anything on him. He's too new to politics. Send out for information about his associates. The slightest irregularity we'll investigate, expand it, and place the blame on Servius. This is, after all, his endeavor."

Servius arrived home in the early evening, tired, but optimistic, and at Scipio's orders. While Servius was free to come and go, there was little he could do to help move things along. Scipio had been impressed to learn that the makeup of the legion had been Servius's doing, but ordered him home nonetheless. As he went through the courtyard, Prisca was there to meet him, and to take his arm.

"There has been good news from well-wishers and the servants moving throughout the city," she explained. "Is it all that good?"

"We have our legion," Servius said, placing his hand over Prisca's. "And all the better for us with Scipio there." They walked along the pool, and came to rest on one of the benches, beside a rose bush that caught the last bit of sunlight in the courtyard.

"Prisca," said Servius, taking her hands in his. "I want to thank you, for last night. For everything. And I want to tell you I'm sorry."

She looked at him, her eyes unknowing.

"I should have been more receptive to you, should have been kinder, more aware. I've been so preoccupied the past few days, and I haven't been able to ask you how you're doing."

"I know I'll be okay," she said, breathing in and out slowly, to steady herself. "When I was lost after running from my home, I wasn't sure I would be okay. Even after I found your villa. But here, right now, with you, I know that I will be."

"And," she added, brushing a lock of hair away from his forehead, "so will you."

She looked at him with honest eyes, tender and searching, soft and dreamlike, the color of the early dawn. And he knew, in that instant, that his heart had given way for her. But, given her emotional situation, and the loss of her home, and her family —her life, really —and if she felt the same way toward him, which she appeared to, then out of respect for her and himself, he knew that whatever existed between them would have to move slowly, if at all for the time being.

They remained there, hands together, until Prisca excused herself to help prepare dinner. As she stood, he kissed her hand, and she held her hand to her lips.

Three days passed, and Servius visited the defense legion's camp daily, as did citizens from the countryside and the city, bringing gifts of food, drink, and common supplies such as bandages and firewood for the troops. By now, the vast number of the residents of all of Italy knew the northern frontier was unguarded, knew there were no troops to send —except these. The force had even earned a popularly-constructed name, the Legia Votum —the Legion of Hope.

"Training is progressing at various levels," revealed Scipio as he, Servius, Titinius, Modius, Titus, and Horatio moved through the camp. "The Emperor's Guard is polished, flawless. The veterans remember their skill and discipline, so not much work has to be done with them. The auxiliaries have the basics down, and are seeking to learn the finer points. But the civilian recruits, like any civilian recruits, have much to learn. We've been interchanging basic drills —handling of weapons, and keeping in file. We're holding our first full-unit drill today, moving from column into line, in various formations."

"I'm impressed," said Servius.

"Don't be," Scipio said. "Apart from the Guard, and the veterans, the rest of this detail might well be a mob."

"You don't have faith they'll manage?"

"With all due respect, I refuse to answer that. I'm here to do a job, and until I've done my job, I can't comment on my faith in possibilities."

"Well," Servius replied. "I have faith in them." A few wagons of supplies arrived, and were being unloaded by members of the Guard. Servius headed toward the wagons, with Scipio behind.

"How is discipline in the camp?" Servius asked, pulling from the wagon a sack of grain, and stacking it alongside where the Guards were doing the same.

"Discipline is good. No deserters, at least not yet. No fights, no quarrels, no complaints, yet." Scipio raised an eyebrow as Servius went for a second sack of grain.

"Is that common?" Servius wondered as he went for a third.

The old general furrowed his brows. "It is isn't uncommon, either –at first. But if this is any indication of how things will turn out, then I think we'll be alright." Scipio, looking around him, noticed that men in the camp were glancing towards the senator, participating in the physical work of piling grain. Some were pointing, and nodding approvingly. It was a good thing that the men saw Servius did not consider himself above them, but of them.

Yet, he felt the need to press the issue.

"Sir, that isn't fitting work for a senator."

"I'm really a farmer," Servius replied, setting down his fifth bag of grain, and completing the unloading. "And besides. What does it matter?"

"Not a thing," Scipio said, realizing he was mildly impressed with the young man —a class apart from most of his peers, and elders.

"Well," Servius said. "I'll return this afternoon after the Senate session. Taxes today."

"Still no word from Numerius?"

"None," said Servius. "I think I'm going to propose a patrol be organized to go up after them, to see if there have been any problems. I'm concerned."

"I'll handle it," said Scipio. "I'll gather together a few trusted men as messengers, and have an answer for you by tomorrow night. I'll also inform the Emperor I am sending them out."

"I appreciate that," said Servius. "Send them out as soon as you can."

Liberius stood on the steps of the curia as senators began arriving for debate the next day. He looked out over the forum, at the people, the rich and the poor, the comings and goings, the passersby, seeking out the face of Cleander as he came through the crowd, his hired bodyguards behind him, for many of the senators had rejected Emperor's Guards as protectors. Keeping a cautious distance from the steps, Cleander's hired men gathered around a monument to Rome's dead generals, slain in combat. Cleander made a beeline for Liberius, keeping his voice low as he spoke.

"Everything is confirmed," Cleander said.

"You're absolutely positive?" Liberius said, his eyes scanning the space around them for prying eyes or listening ears.

"Yes. My men went to visit Capito's armory offices while he wasn't home, to discover a contract for weapons had been drawn up the night he arrived in

Rome. You were right when you said to look at Servius's associates. They've been planning to raise a legion. Between what they have out on the Cassian Way, and the Emperor's Guard, they could overthrow the Emperor or the Senate, or both –or, at least, that's what we can claim."

"Very good," Liberius said. "Well done."

"So shall I confront him on the floor?"

Liberius bit his lower lip, his mind in deep thought. At last, he said, "No."

"No?"

"No," said Liberius. "We want to make a spectacle of this. The Senate is one thing, but the people are another. Have your men spread the word that there is to be a public gathering at Aurelian Field to celebrate the progress the Legion of Hope has made so far. And then you and I will arrive conveniently at the same time to confront Servius with the dealings of his associates, in front of not only the pitiful mock military unit he has hammered together, but in front of the wretched rabble of this city. His humiliation will be absolute; and we will hire men to arrest him there in front of the world."

"The Senate adjourns far too much, I think," said Servius as he arrived home at noon, taking Prisca's hands in his. "I'm glad to see you."

She smiled, felt heat rising in her face, knew that Servius saw the rose blush of her cheeks, and couldn't resist smiling again because of it.

"I'm glad to see you," she said. "How was Scipio this morning? And the legion?"

"They're coming along. Scipio is well. He certainly seems alive for the task at hand."

Prisca bowed her arm in Servius's as they headed through the courtyard. "Will you go and see them again today?" she wondered.

"I will indeed."

"Good," she said. "I have heard, walking through the forum earlier, that there will be a large turnout of people from the city today to the camp, to see what strides the legion has made."

"I wonder who organized that?"

"I don't think anyone knows," said Prisca. "But the people are certainly excited about it."

Servius let out a small laugh. "I doubt that Scipio will like it very much. He'll probably form the legion and have them chase away the observers as a drill."

Prisca let her forehead rest on Servius's shoulder—and she laughed. It was a sound that caught both she and Servius off guard. It was a beautiful, warm, and soul rising sound, like the voice of a long-missed loved one, or the sound of birds in the early spring, or of music that propelled the heart to indescribable transcendence.

It was the first time she had laughed since the night she had come to his estate, at least to Servius's knowledge.

"I shall remember this," Servius said, touching her cheek. "The day that sunlight appeared once more in your eyes."

The afternoon sunlight fell down on the Roman countryside like a veil of light, luminescent, radiant, warming. Servius, followed closely by Titus and Horatio, Orianus, Vespius, and their guards, were cheered as they rode past the people making their way to Aurelian Field.

"This may be the longest-sustained popularity of a senator," Orianus jokingly said. "Such popularity is a blessing, and a curse."

"Oh dear goodness," Vespius said. "You've become a philosopher. First there was Plato's Republic. Then Cicero's. Now Orianus's."

"No," said Orianus lightheartedly, and in respect. "The Rome we now speak of belongs to Servius."

But Servius, riding ahead, did not hear the compliment. The entire legion was lined up on Aurelian Field, the unit's newly-crafted gold standard glistening in the sun. Scipio, Titinius, and Modius sat astride horses, conferring with one another, probably about the public exodus to the camp. The three military officers met Servius and his group at the road.

"I trust that this is not your doing?" Scipio said, looking confused and angry.

"I had nothing to do with this," said Servius.

"I don't care who is responsible for this," said Scipio. "While I appreciate the enthusiasm of those people, I cannot conduct my role or the legion properly with these sorts of distractions."

"I'll see about some private farmland well off of Cassian," said Servius apologetically —but as he spoke, the sound of horse hooves beating the cobbled roads like thunder, stole the attention of everyone present. From down the lane now came a mass of perhaps fifty armed, mounted men, with Liberius and Cleander at the head.

"What is this?" Orianus wondered aloud.

Liberius reigned in his horse, posturing himself between the people and Servius, and taking note of Scipio.

"I'm surprised to see you without your face in a gutter," Liberius said to the general.

"I'm surprised to see you without your face in one, either," said Scipio.

"Insolent, foolish wit," said Liberius. He became louder. "I am putting an end to this treacherous activity now!" He stood up in the stirrups, so the people could see him. "People of Rome! You have been deceived by Senator Servius!" There was some booing, but Liberius went on. "Consider if you will this military force he has assumed responsibility for! Supposedly, it was put together to defend Rome!"

Servius leaned forward in his saddle, fear, anxiety, anger, and curiosity raging in his soul.

"People of Rome! Servius did not put together this military force to defend the city, but to overthrow it! I have evidence to prove it! He means to imprison the Senate and murder the Emperor, our beloved Majorian! Consider if you will that an ambitious Senator, and a drunkard of an ex-general would conspire together to supplant your government!"

"Stay your tongue!" shouted Scipio, drawing his sword.

"Even now the villain seeks to move against me!" shouted Liberius, pointing to Scipio. "What treachery! What treason! Last week, before the Senate convened, these villains —Servius, Orianus, and Vespius —were seeking revolution! They secretly made a pact with an armorer for weapons, uniforms, and armor before the Senate even convened to grant that a legion could be raised! They were preparing to arm a legion that did not yet exist! They have been preparing for this for God knows how long!"

The crowed was silent; Scipio was enraged; Orianus and Vespius both looked helpless. Servius urged his horse out slightly ahead of them.

"Liberius, what on earth are you doing?" Yet it suddenly made sense to Servius. The public turnout, Liberius's stellar arrival with hired men –and the pragmatic tendencies of Orianus and Vespius had finally come back to haunt them.

"I plan to go to the Emperor himself with this knowledge!" shouted Liberius. "I will bring the traitors before Majorian and reveal their hideous, barbarian-worthy plot!" Now, he turned to the men behind him. "As Senator, I hereby order you to retrieve the traitors, and arrest them! Begin with the mastermind, Servius!"

The mounted thugs behind Liberius and Cleander began to move forward toward Servius, yet as they did so, there was a great commotion behind him. Before the thugs could reach Servius, soldiers from the legion –Emperor's Guards, veterans, auxiliaries, the archers from the circus, and dozens of others, led by Quintus Decinius –rushed forward to place themselves between Servius and Liberius's men. Among them were Titus and Horatio. Behind Servius, the rest of the legion formed a protective barrier around Scipio and the others. The thugs, outnumbered hopelessly, halted their horses.

Liberius turned to the people watching. "Do you see!" he shouted. "They are all in on this! Every single one of them!"

But for the people on the hill –many of them friends and family of those in the legion –Liberius had now gone one step too far. They began shouting, began condemning Liberius, began cursing him and mocking him.

More horse hooves slammed against the paved road, and another party stormed down the Cassian Way. Cheers then went up as the people realized who was coming: the Emperor and his mounted Guard. Liberius's face was red, either from anger, or embarrassment; Cleander's face was white. The thugs they had hired looked at one another, and around them with nervous eyes.

Majorian reared his horse up between Servius and Liberius, and his Guard stood by, prepared to defend the Emperor.

"People of Rome!" shouted Majorian. "I am not sure what has happened here to confuse our friend Liberius, but I want you to know this: The legion on Aurelian Field is here with the blessing of the Senate, and my full support and approval. Do return home with happy hearts and comfort in the knowledge that this has all been a tremendous misunderstanding! We are all here at your service!"

A roaring ovation went up from the crowd, and Majorian dismounted his horse, gesturing both Servius and Liberius to do the same. With the Emperor present, the legion returned to formation, and the Emperor's personal Guard took over the duty of protecting their imperial leader and senators.

"Well," said Majorian. "When half the city is missing, it isn't difficult to find out where they've gone. And when a senator rides through the Palatine with a band of armed thugs, they aren't hard to follow."

Liberius said nothing, gritted his teeth, and folded his arms.

"Senator Liberius... I'm not sure what you were trying to accomplish here. But surely you've only misunderstood what has been going on. In fact, I trust in your wisdom and your judgment —and your loyalty not to oppose me —that I can accept that this has all been a severe misunderstanding. I would hate for the Senate to learn that this has been the result of a personal vendetta, that a regal senator should consort with common criminals to attempt to undo a fellow senator, who is himself in service to the people of Rome. So please, do tell me this has been a misunderstanding." Majorian's voice was calm, but laced with the threat of danger.

Liberius drew in a sharp breath. "It has been a misunderstanding, Majesty," Liberius said. "It was my own fault." He looked at Servius, and nearly choked on the words that followed. "I apologize for this."

"I am glad to hear that," Majorian said. "Just as I shall be glad to hear that you'll propose in session tomorrow that we increase funding for military affairs."

Liberius practically seethed, nearly spitting in anger, yet relenting. "Of course, Majesty. For the good of Rome."

"Always for Rome," Majorian said. "Now, pay your men, and disband them. And make sure Cleander recognizes that our defense budget will begin increasing tomorrow."

"I shall be happy to carry the message, my Emperor," said Liberius, bowing and returning to his horse.

As Liberius and Cleander left, and as their group broke up, Majorian approached Vespius, Orianus, and Scipio. Servius, and Decinius stood beside the Emperor.

"You appear to have earned the legion's loyalty," said Majorian, to the old general. "And that is a good thing."

"And my loyalty is to Rome," Scipio said gruffly. "And to you."

"I'm not worried about the military," Majorian said, putting Scipio at ease. "Remember... they put me on the throne. It is the Senate that I must win over. Thanks to Liberius's roughshod attempt at usurping more power for himself, he finds himself suddenly unable to oppose me in the curia. I do believe you'll have no more trouble from Liberius. I do however want to take this opportunity to inform you that we have received, by way of signal fires, news that our messengers are racing back. They'll be here tonight. I will be convening the Senate when they arrive."

"Tonight, then," said Servius as Majorian returned to his horse.

"And Servius," Majorian added. "Good show."

Meeting by torchlight in the curia, the Roman Imperial Senate awaited, in quiet and tense anticipation, the entry of the messengers sent out to see about Numerius. The marble of the meeting house adopted wintry blue shadows and fire orange light, in continual competition with one another as the torches burned. The windows of the curia were dark; and Majorian stood before his throne beneath them. Scipio and Servius stood behind Majorian, along with Ricimer. Liberius sat in his place, looking shrunken and sheepish.

"Bring him in," ordered the Emperor.

Two guards opened the doors, and in came a dust-covered, scruffy, and clearly exhausted man named Vitus. He adjusted the tunic beneath his armor, and he came to kneel before the Majorian, who bade the man to rise.

"What have you to report?"

The man drew in a deep breath, and Servius noticed then that his left arm was bloodied and bandaged.

"As commanded by General Scipio, we rode hard north, switching our mounts as we rode. We passed through Colonia Caesarium, and I conferred with Senator Orianus's friend and the commander of the local forces, Tertius, who confirmed that Numerius's party had passed through a few days previous.

"We rode north into the mountains. The smaller passes were overcome by the snow that had previously fallen, so we took the main passage from the Aquilan Valley that went through the town of Colonia Aquilo. We continued on through the main pass, to the heights overlooking the next valley. At the time, a passing snowstorm blinded our view below, but on the descending slope, we found Numerius's party."

Liberius looked especially anxious, leaning forward in his seat.

"Numerius and his entire escort are dead," Vitus revealed. "They were massacred. There were a handful of dead opponents around them —all of them Goths. Numerius… we identified him only by the shreds of fabric he still wore. He and his company were hacked apart, mutilated. The snow around them had melted from the heat of their blood.

"As we went back up to the heights, the storm lessened, and we could see in the valley below us an ocean of men and tents, under the banner of Rufus. We could see, in the distant passes, more Gothic columns advancing, coming to join him. They are forming up inside the mountains of Italy. It's clear what they intend to do. On our way out, a Goth patrol came upon us, and we had to fight to get back."

Liberius said nothing, would not look up now, knew then what was expected of him —though he wanted nothing more to shout, to scream, to condemn, to wield the power he had lost. The curia was in an uproar, senators shouting and talking and gesturing.

"The choice is clear," Majorian said loudly. "Tomorrow, Sevius and Scipio will lead their men into the mountains to defend the pass at Colonia Aquila, and northern Italy in the process."

Servius acquiesced to Scipio, who stepped forward. "We will leave at dawn," he said. The Senate broke out into an applause.

"Noble Emperor," Liberius said halfheartedly, rising. "I propose, that, in the absence of the legion of Servius and Scipio, that we in the Senate... increase... defense funding."

"That is a remarkable idea," seconded Vespius. "I believe it is time for the state to raise and arm new legions." The response was in the affirmative and overwhelming.

"I likewise suggest," said Majorian, stepping forward himself and taking the floor, "that the XIV Legion, under the command of General Valerus, be recalled from the western front, to meet with and reinforce Servius and Scipio at Colonia Aquilo. I have been in contact with Valerus, and his front is quiet and can, if needed, be defended by the three legions that remain on that frontier. It is a dangerous move, but we will need to take the risk to defend our center. Yet, I will not issue the orders without the Senate's consent."

The Senate voiced its approval loudly, and thunderously —and both Servius and Liberius understood that the Emperor was making a power play. For Servius, it was the restoration of political justice; for Liberius, the dimming prospects of his own ends.

"Then I shall send word at once to have Valerus's XIV Legion converge with and join Servius and Scipio," Majorian announced. "With the new legions to be raised, we will be able to properly man and defend our borders!"

The ovation was deafening.

Returning home, Servius paced the courtyard twice, considering what it was that he should pack —or if he should pack anything at all. It was late; everyone else was asleep, except for Titus, who had gone to see his family, and Horatio, who was at the armory to sharpen his sword and knife —and neither one were present. When they both returned, they would set out for Aurelian Field.

Servius at last decided on a single, small trunk, with extra clothing, his own copy of the Vulgate, his cross, and some papers for dispatches. He also went to the large trunk at the foot of his bed, and pulled from the interior the sword of his grandfather, who had served as commander of a cohort during the Civil War of 394. Servius had little practice with a sword, and no experience with the spear or the bow —yet he was determined to bring the sword anyway, just in case.

Returning to the courtyard, Servius found Prisca, sitting by herself on one of the stone benches. She was pale, and trembled slightly, and it reminded Servius of the first time he had seen her. He approached her carefully, and she did not look up at him.

"Is it true," she whispered quietly. "You're leaving?"

Servius nodded. Prisca didn't look up to see him affirm the truth she already knew.

"When will you be back?"

"As soon as the situation with Rufus is handled," he said.

A single tear rolled down her cheek. "Just as I was starting to come to peace," she said.

"I'm sorry," Servius said, sitting beside her. She put her head against his neck and closed her eyes, and he felt her tears on his chest, against his heart. He brought his cloak around both of them, and held her tight; and the night wind stirred the flowers of the garden, and brought the smell of roses to them. She trembled against him; he protected her from the night wind.

"Please be safe," she said. "Please."

"I will be," Servius said.

"I can't lose you," she said, reaching up and touching his lips. There was the sound of horses outside, and Servius knew his time was short.

"I'll be back here, just as soon as I can be. I'll write to you," he said.

"Just make sure you come back," Prisca pleaded as Titus and Horatio appeared at the gate. She quickly put into Servius's hand a white scarf, one she had purchased for him. "Remember me by this," she said.

Prisca stood, and Servius with her. Gently, he brushed away her tears from her eyes with his thumb, and he placed his lips on her forehead, softly; and Prisca retreated into her room, taking with her his heart.

Opening the gate to the house, Servius stood aside as Titus and Horatio brought in a wooden crate. "This," said Titus as he opened the box, "is from the Emperor, with his respects; and it has been blessed by the Pope."

Inside the box lay an officer's military uniform, chest plate, helmet, and sword and scabbard. Servius changed quickly, but substituted the new sword for his grandfather's.

"I trust the Emperor would not mind," he commented to Titus and Horatio, both of whom concurred that Majorian would not.

"I suppose, then, that we should be on our way."

Titus loaded up Servius's small trunk into the carriage, and Servius turned to take one last look around. It was not home, but it was home —Prisca had made it home —and now he would be leaving it, perhaps forever.

"God," he whispered into the wind, "please bless this house, and all those in it, and all those homes tonight that will lose loved ones to this campaign. Deliver us from evil, and bless our endeavors. Help us to stand."

IX

Emperor Majorian watched with his mounted Guard from the hill overlooking Aurelian Field as the Legia Votum broke in camp, and put to column on the road in the near darkness. The air was still and cold, and the breath of the men and horses could be dimly seen. There had been no time for a public ceremony to send the legion off, no time for a parade, no time for anything. Even now, riders were enroute to Valerus, riding all night, switching mounts, being preceded by signal torches.

In the Senate that day, Orianus and Vespius would officially press for new legions to be raised, and capable commanders would be sought out for them as the call for volunteers to fill the ranks would go out. If God was truly on their side, then everything could be done: the western frontier would not be pushed in absence of the XIV Legion, and the Servius and Scipio would stop Rufus for the time being. And Liberius would remain as he was: defanged and holding onto the shredded consciousness that was his pride.

The red uniforms and bronze armor of the Legion of Hope could be seen now, in the dark gray light; the stomp of feet, the cling of metal, the clamp of hooves and the grinding of wagon wheels against the road; Rome sending forth her sons once more to defend territory that should never have been compromised. And in the gray dawn, the mist and the fog that covered the spring fields and the valleys, Rome herself trembled – and there was Rome, a farming community, fighting for its life; and then a town, growing and seeking influence; and then mighty city reaching out into the world, and then the most powerful force on Earth in the history of the world up to that time, that was now fighting for its very existence once more. The infant, and the elder, survival a dream, a hope, a prayer –the apex of existence at the nadir; survival the only possible path, and it had to be taken.

"God be with you all," said Majorian quietly as he turned his horse around to return to the Empire.

By noon, there were more than two hundred stragglers, most of them volunteers. Scipio had briefly entertained the thought of moving on with an advance element of all those who could keep up, and waiting for the rest in camp by that night –but then decided against it, wanting to keep the force together in the event they did not reach the pass before Rufus decided to move through it. Then, they would need every man available.

Servius rode his horse, and walked among the men at various times, speaking to them, getting to know who they were; at other times, he went on ahead with the forward guards. His presence, Scipio noticed, encouraged the men –and morale was important. Yet, Scipio could not hide his own frustration with the aggravatingly slow pace much of the legion was adopting. He had hoped to be in position the night of the fifth day; and now it appeared as if they would not arrive until the sixth day. There was no telling how long the snow storm would keep Rufus at bay. Scipio explained these frustrations to Servius.

"The consequences of this are that we won't be in position in time to defend against Rufus," Scipio revealed. "We're outnumbered."

"Even with the XIV Legion?" Scipio asked.

"I'm acting as if they shall not arrive in time," Scipio said, handing Servius a map of the mountains. "I want to be on good defensive positions on the high ground at the narrowest part of the pass near Colonia Aquilo. We'll use the geographic advantages to offset our numbers –like the Spartans and their allies against the Persians at Thermopylae. We'll have the narrowness of the pass, the slope of the high ground, and the ground of our own choosing and study. But we have to get there first. What we cannot afford is a pitched battle out in the open. There, Rufus will be able to use his cavalry to deadly ends; for our own part, we have only two hundred cavalrymen, from the Emperor's Guard cohort. They will not be enough to counter whatever Rufus throws at us –unless we have that pass."

"Have you explained this to the men?" Servius posited.

"I have not," said Scipio. "Spies can appear to be the most loyal of men."

"You don't have to give them the details," Servius responded. "Tell them what is at stake. Tell them that we have to pick up our pace. Tell them our lives depend on it. They will listen to you. I'm sure there will still be stragglers, but that can't be helped. When it comes down to it, they'll be on the lines as well."

Scipio regarded the young senator for a moment, adjusting the white scarf around his neck, impressed once more.

"Perhaps I will speak to them," the old general said. "When we stop for rest, I will ride among the men, to each cohort, and exhort them to better performance."

"It can't hurt," said Servius.

As the column drew to rest, Scipio went out to the cohorts composed of auxiliaries and volunteers, knowing the volunteers would need the most work. He sat astride his horse, the portrait of an aged, career soldier, a warrior for Rome, and he raised his hand in the air.

"Men of Rome," he announced. "I applaud your discipline, and your determination to go out on behalf of Rome to defend her, and all that you hold dear. But I must ask of you this task, that you set out once more, keeping a quick, lively, and orderly pace, and keeping your columns together. It is difficult work, I know. For years, I fought among the ranks. I bled and sacrificed. I marched over mountains and through valleys, waded across rivers and stormed citadels. I met the enemy in open ground, and on the streets of villages. Soldiering is not easy. But every advantage we can muster to our cause makes the act of soldiering that much less difficult. And what we need now is speed, the swiftness of foot. I implore you to make haste as much as you can —and then push yourself to do better. Time is precious, and we must covet every instant."

The soldiers watched the great general, his red cape flowing in the afternoon wind; the white horse upon which he sat bowed his head, as though in deference to his rider. There, they knew of the exhortations of Caesar, to bring his men across the Rubicon in the march on Rome; here, they knew of a man condemned and cast away by the Senate, now the only commander capable of preventing a barbarian march on Rome.

They talked among one another after the great general had gone from their presence to other cohorts; they talked about their blistered feet and their aching legs, of their shoulders worn from carrying their spears. And they talked about home. They talked about home and love and everything that made them leave their trades, their families —they talked about everything worth risking their lives for. If not them, then who? There was no one else. Every generation is faced with dark times, with the gravest crises and dangers and emergencies; this they knew. And so, if the great general needed more speed, they would find a way to do that, pushing themselves to their limits —and then redefining new limits to break. The mantle was theirs to take; the torch was theirs to carry against the darkness.
Father Marcellus, who had accompanied the expedition, went among the cohorts, following Scipio, blessing the troops, and praying with them. God had chosen them for this task, it seemed.

The army resumed marching; by nightfall, they had exceeded their goal for the first day by three miles. It was an unexpected improvement.

"The days have changed," Scipio said to Servius that night. "Once, Roman generals had stragglers whipped. Now they are kept in check by hope. But," the old man added gruffly, "hope won't keep them alive. Hope won't stop Rufus."

"Well," said Servius. "That's what we have you for."

Scipio shook his head, and laughed a little. "Oh God," he said. "If we had a senate full of men like you... And if our military was half of what it once was..."

"It will be that way again," Servius said.

Scipio threw a stick into the fire before them. "You really do believe that... Everything."

"You know... I'm not sure you don't believe that, either."

Scipio laughed. "I'm too old to believe in anything but God."

"That's a starting point, then," said Servius.

Scipio laughed again, and turned in for the night. Servius remained before the fire, stretching out his hands toward the warmth; closing his eyes, he remembered the warmth of Prisca's fingertips against his lips, the incandescent light of her eyes. It had been less than two weeks since he had left his home, had gone to Rome, had served in the Senate, had befriended the Emperor and put in command of a legion. What would the morning bring, he wondered. What would the morning bring? Would Rufus remain in his valley camp with the snow? Or were they already coming down from the mountains? Would he, and Scipio, and their men all be mutilated after they had been massacred?

In the morning, the legion broke camp and moved out, back along the Cassian Way. Beyond the advance guard, Scipio had decided to send out four men in peasant clothing to scout ahead, all the way up to Colonia Aquilo, and then to report back either as soon as they encountered Rufus's army, or as soon as they were confident that Rufus would remain where he was in the valley.

The night of the fourth day, half of the scouting party returned. They reported that Rufus was still embedded in his valley camp, that snow had made the main pass difficult to traverse at best, but that warm winds were sweeping up from the south —a change in weather that could melt the snow and give Rufus a clear shot to Colonia Aquilo. The citizens of the town had been taking watch over the encampment, it was reported, and they had sent word out to the transalpine cohort —the same one that had been massacred —so no response had ever come. Two of the scouts had stayed behind, to keep an eye on the enemy.

"And the people of the town?" Servius asked the scout.

"Most of them are terrified. They were planning to leave, but the snow storm kept them as well."

"Did you tell them anything about us?" Scipio asked, always concerned about spies.

"Not a word," said the scout. "We posed as travelers seeking to see about the Gallic estate of a senator."

"Good," Scipio said. He looked over his map. "We'll make Aquilo by tomorrow evening, once we head up out of the valley here. And Rufus will be forced to come straight at us."

"Why wouldn't Rufus take a side pass?" Servius inquired.

"The snow worked in our favor up until this moment, keeping Rufus stationary. The melting snow will make the passes muddy, meaning heavy equipment – such as catapults –will be impossible to move up the mountain. The mud will slow down the advance of their infantry and their cavalry. And if they do decide to use cavalry, their ability to charge –between moving uphill and having to contend with the mud –will be greatly diminished, if not altogether entirely undone. But all of this means we have to reach Aquilo by tomorrow."

The legion was rousted two hours earlier the following morning, and moved out in the dark, slow and steady past Colonia Caesarium; the pace was quickened as the son arched high overhead. The pool of stragglers increased to more than four hundred men, and Marcellus remained with them, to encourage them.

Slowly, the land rose; farmhouses and villas appeared amid the fields and crops among the earth; patches of wood, of deciduous and evergreen trees, dotted the landscape and followed the courses of mountain streams. Snow covered more and more of the ground as the column travelled over the arduous ground beneath a gray sky.

Eventually, the valley narrowed and became a pass, one which led to the plateau that the town of Colonia Aquilo was built upon. Smoke rose from the fireplaces of the small homes, drawn out by tubes built into the walls of the buildings, which themselves sat huddled together beneath the snow of the previous few days. As the legion appeared, at the edge of town, the sun broke through the clouds, and fell across the men, lifting their spirits –and causing many of the villages to look through windows and come out of their homes, faces full of relief and happiness.

"Thank God you've come!"

"We thought no one would answer our calls!"

"Welcome! Welcome!"

"God bless you! God bless you all!"

Scipio scanned the landscape around him. The town was situated in the northern half of the plateau, which became the Aquilan Slope –a steady decline into the pass. Northwest of the town were mines used to extract ore for iron; to the south was a lumber camp for the pine forests around the town. South of the lumber camp was a path used by woodcutters, which ran back down to the valley. West of the town was an old mining pass, one which twisted and turned at breakneck angles back toward the main pass two miles on. It was near this old pass, between the lumber camp and the mines, and just beyond the town that Scipio decided to make camp.

Scipio rode past the arriving men, to find Decinius, at the head of the Emperor's Guard.

"It appears as if we've made it, General Scipio," Decinius saluted.

"We have. Keep your men in ranks, and then deploy on the slope. Send out scouts to observe Rufus. Your men will be joined shortly by the veteran cohort, while the rest of the legion quickly makes camp. Once your scouts return, report to me at once, and we'll determine what to do from there."

Scipio then sought out Titinius, to round up some of the locals for information about the pass and the area. Two villagers –the town's magistrate, Antonius, and the head of the woodcutting industry, Felix, volunteered to come and talk to Scipio.

Antonius, an elderly man, explained that much of the snow had melted, and the warm weather of the day would probably melt much of the rest of the snow, at least on the floor of the pass, for such spring storms were common there. Felix went on to explain that an old mining trail connected both the old mining pass, and the area of the mines, back when Aquilo was little more than a handful of shacks. It was used mainly by children in town to play, and was unknown except to locals.

Servius, meanwhile, rode with Titus, Horatio, and Decinius to the Aquilan Slope with the cohort of Emperor's Guards.

The land fell away before them, between two mountains, capped with snow and bright against the sky. Thickly forested by pine and fir, with a collection of deciduous trees here and there, the landscape might never have had man set foot upon it, untouched, eternal.

"It is either of great irony, or poetic justice, that this is where we make our stand," Servius said as the scouts headed down the hill, and the cohort formed.

A moment later, Scipio arrived with Modius, and the two joined Servius and Decinius. Scipio quickly looked out across the ground, and nodded. "This will do." He then turned to Modius. "Round up every soldier who isn't exhausted, and ask for volunteers from the town, especially the woodcutters. I want the bottom of the hill covered with tree trunks, sharpened like stakes, pointing toward Rufus. I want holes dug at random between the stakes, as deep as can be done. That way, any assault they launch against us, either with cavalry or infantry, will be broken up and disorganized before it reaches our front line. I also want trees felled and formed into barricades at the crest of the hill, for archers to fire from."

Modius saluted. "Yes, sir!"

Within twenty minutes, a hundred volunteers from the town had been rounded up, along with eight hundred soldiers, and they set to work at once on the slope. A few hours later, the messengers returned to confirm that Rufus was still in camp, but the camp was being organized for moving out. In all probability, Rufus would move up the mountain in the morning.

"Seeing the slope of the land," Scipio explained, "he will be forced to attack, or retreat. The other passes are too narrow, too difficult to use effectively, either in snow or in mud. Therefore, he will be forced to commit his troops here, because here has the best chance of deploying the most men he can, in as broad a front as he can. And here is where will break them."

The work on the slop continued into the early evening. Soldiers who had rested exchanged shifts with those working since arriving. Dinner was prepared, tents had been thrown up, and smaller logs were secured by the woodcutters for the soldiers to use on for floors in their shelters.

Scipio also received word that Valerus's XIV Legion was still on the march, that it had had to remain in position while its neighboring legions made up for the gap it would leave in the lines. Valerus could be expected the following night —too late for the battle, unless the battle extended beyond one day. But it was news that Scipio ordered kept between the messenger and Servius, so as not to concern the members of their own force.
At dusk, Servius found himself at the head of the old mining pass, along with Horatio, Titus, and Scipio.

"Shouldn't we do anything about this?" Servius asked of the steep, winding, and elongated path, still mostly covered with heavy snow.

Scipio let his eyes travel along the path, along the folds and crevices of the mountains, at the snakelike route of the pass.

"Rufus would be an idiot to attempt to commit himself to this course," Scipio announced. "He will use the main pass for his attack."

"What about a diversion?" Servius pressed.

"He wouldn't be able to spare men taking the main pass," Scipio replied. "Either he commits himself fully and totally here, or he withdraws into Gaul. But let us say, for the sake of argument, that Rufus did move his army through this side pass. It would be a matter of the greatest ease to reform our lines here. A hundred men could keep Rufus's whole army in check here, at least for a while. But again, we have no worries of that."

Following dinner, Scipio called his officers to his tent, to go over the formations for the morning. As Servius, Titinius, Modius, Decinius, and the other cohort commanders stood about him, Scipio made marks and drew his plans up on the map between them all.

"The Emperor's Guard will form the core of the defense tomorrow," Scipio revealed. "They will form the front ranks, divided up into three large groups. Two hundred in the center group, and one hundred in both the left and right groups. The remaining two hundred Guards –those who brought mounts –will remain by their horses, either to stem a breakthrough, God forbid, or to be used as reserves to bolster the lines.

"Behind the front ranks of Guards, the veterans will fall into position, one hundred men to each group. The reserves will fall in behind them, four hundred men to each group. The three cohorts of auxiliaries will form secondary groups behind the main groups. The cohort of gladiators, and the volunteers, will form a third line with the archers at the log barricades. A handful of them will also remain in the camp to guard it against any local thieves. Are there any questions?"

"None," said Decinius.

"Alright then. Divide up the cohorts, reorganize them into their respective groups, and make sure your men are familiar with their group number, so any tactical moves can be made as necessary."

"It will be done," Titinius said as the meeting broke up.

Servius, moving across the cold earth to his tent, came across Felix, the woodcutter, sitting on the stump of a freshly-downed tree. He bore a look of contempt and dejection on his face, so much so that Servius stopped to speak to him.

"What are you thinking?" Servius asked.

Felix spit into the snow. "I'm not sure you'd want to hear it."

"I'm a senator," Servius said kindly. "I'm always interested in what people have to say."

"Ha! A senator! That's wonderful. So tell me, Senator... Tell me... what happens at the end of the day?"

"I'm not sure I follow?" Servius said, folding his arms.

"To us, to the Empire! What happens tomorrow? What happens twenty years from today? How much longer is Rome going to fight the rest of the world? How much longer is Rome going to look for places to conquer, to spread its influence? Why are Romans never satisfied?"

"Are you a Roman?" Servius asked.

"Yes," said Felix. "But I'm not sure that I like it."

"We're not here to conquer anything," Servius said. "We're here to stop those barbarian from coming up through the pass."

"And why are they coming through the pass, Senator?" The word senator was spewed with visceral hatred. But before Servius could answer, Felix went on. "I'll tell you why. Because we've spent the last thousand years pillaging and raping and murdering and slaughtering and enslaving. Because we got rich from it all, and we didn't give the slightest concern to the girls we raped or the houses we burned down or the people we murdered. Well, Senator, I've got news for you. I have two daughters —one is twelve, one is fourteen —and if the Goths come up over that hill, I'll kill my daughters so the Goths won't be able to touch them. I'll burn down my own house so that the Goths won't have the pleasure of doing it themselves.

"They're in that valley over there, dreaming of treasure and riches and power, dreaming of revenge and rape and murder because they want what Rome has, what Rome once took from them. And we are no different from them. They hate us because our soldiers are in their lands, because of everything we've done to them."

"That is precisely where you're wrong," Servius said. "Rome may not have an immaculate history, but find for me the race of people or the nation who is without some kind of sin. That doesn't justify our failings, and it doesn't excuse them either. But what we have to offer the world is something never before seen, not even when Alexander lived."

"And so you will kill and burn to spread civilization?"

"Civilization does not always come at the sharp end of the sword," Servius responded swiftly. "There are innumerable peoples who, now and in the past, have voluntarily aligned themselves with us, have sought to learn from us, have sought to become part of our Empire –and remain loyal to it. We have brought the world a better chance of stability. We have brought to the world the brightest annals of Greek learning, and our own original philosophy and knowledge. We have brought the world modern medicine and architecture, art and theater, coliseums and circuses, paved roads and internal plumbing, aqueducts and baths, trade and wealth, literacy and music, and above all, the message and religion of Jesus Christ.

"So let me ask you, Felix, if you would prefer that we were here, or not?"

"I have no choice in the matter," said Felix. "I am a woodcutter."

"And you a free man," Servius said, his passion strengthening. "You, through the Grace of God Almighty, have been born into a free world, and you enjoy freedom like no other. You're not down in Rufus's camp; you're up here. If you truly believe that Rome is that horrible of a place, nothing is stopping you from running for office, from assisting the Church, from doing something that can improve the problems you find. Better that, than sitting here in love with your own self-pity and bitterness, or scoffing at the people for trying something where you will not."

Felix began laughing, and Servius was unsure of what to say. Titus and Horatio came to stand defensively by Servius as Felix stood up.

"Well, Senator," Felix said in between guffaws, "I've got to hand it to you. You're certainly honest, and that's so original, it's hysterical!"

"Show some respect," Horatio growled, but Servius waved him off.

"An honest senator," Felix laughed, heading toward home. "Honest!"

"What was wrong with that man?" Horatio asked.

"He's lost hope, at the very least," Servius said gravely.

"More like his mind," said Scipio, stepping up beside them. "He's all courageous and brash so long as there's a legion around. I wonder if he had emerged from his house at all since the Goths filled up the valley... Shall we go and sit before a fire?"

The two men made their way toward the closest fire, where Titinius was also present.

"How is everything?" Servius asked.

"The preparations are finished," Scipio revealed. "All that we wait on now is Rufus."

"Will we hold him back?"

"We will," Scipio said, nodding.

"Do you ever get nervous before battle?"

"I don't have the time," Scipio said, noticing that perhaps the younger man was anxious. "But, when I was younger, and fighting in line –I was."

Servius nodded.

"The truth is," Scipio went on, "I'd rather stare down the hordes than fellow senators. I have no idea how someone like you can manage Liberius without putting a sword through his chest. And Liberius is like that woodcutter idiot who claims Roman outposts invite danger rather than keep order. Liberius succeeded in having a number of such outposts in Gaul removed, only for the area to descend into chaos thereafter, and Roman families living in the region raped, slain, and held hostage by their own rebels, and by barbarians. If all we're supposedly doing is harm, then why do so many people seek out our help, militarily, financially, morally? We constantly self-improve. It's one of the things associated with never being satisfied as Romans."

Servius smiled, nodding. "You're right." He then looked up at the older general.

"Why did you, honestly, decide to accept my request to join this legion?"

"To be honest," Scipio said, raising his hands to the fire, "I hadn't intended to lead at all. The thought of pay was the first thing to get me thinking that perhaps I should lead. And then, what you said, about honor... And the fact that I figured I owed it to your father. Did he ever tell you how I came to know him?"

"All he ever said about you," recalled Scipio, "was that you were incredibly brave, that you fought gallantly, that you had as much expertise on the field as Aetius, and that you were loyal to Rome herself above all."

Scipio nodded. "Three years ago, Valerus was my second-in-command of the XIV Legion. Then I was transferred east. There was the threat of war, you remember, between the factions of Valentinian, Petronius Maximus, and Avitus, which began a quick succession of emperors, and profound instability for two years. At the end of those two years, in December, Majorian was elevated by the armed forces to the throne, with that barbarian general, Ricimer's support. You see, I was in command of the entire eastern front during the war —three full legions of experienced troops —and I refused to get involved in the struggle for the throne. I kept my legions in their positions, and when Petronius Maximus was enthroned, I was called before the Senate.

"The Senate censured me, and stripped me of everything I had, from my military honors to my home. There were only a handful of senators who defended my decision not to become involved. The most vocal was your father. I listened to him chastise the Senate, telling them I valued Rome's security above personal gain —but our friend Liberius was able to convince the Senate that I was a coward for not committing to any side in the struggle.

"After that session, your father died of a heart attack. I attended the funeral for him in disguise. And I watched you give his eulogy in the forum. I was impressed, and moved. But the last two years... I somehow lost sight of things. Until a certain young Senator reminded me what was what, and what was at stake. And here I am."

"Hopefully I'm not just some ancient dreamer with unrealistic expectations."

"You saw the people who turned out to volunteer. What do you think they think?"

Servius bowed his head, eyes on the fire. "Perhaps there are still more than just a few dreamers left." Servius returned his gaze to Scipio.

"Were you ever married?"

"I was. A long time ago."

"What happened?"

"I was eighteen when I was married," Scipio said. "My wife was a few years younger. We both lived in one of the poorer sections of Rome. I was part of the reserves. When the Visigoths sacked Rome in 410... Well... My wife didn't survive. I was on the walls, she was part of a column of refugees that was struck by a fireball from a Visigoth catapult. And then from there I decided that it would be in the active service that I would make my life."

"I'm sorry," Servius said in sympathy, thinking of Prisca. "What was your wife's name?"

"Aemilia." The old general's face, weary a moment before, was full of love in his remembrance. "I'll be seeing her again," he added. "Sooner rather than later, I'm sure... Servius... If you ever find the right woman... Don't hesitate to steal her heart."

"If that's an order," said Servius, "then it is one I'll take." He held Prisca's white scarf between his hands firmly, but gently.

Scipio laughed a little. "Then consider it an order." He stood, stiffly, his body weary, his heart heavy. "I'm off to see about the switching of the watch. And then I'm going to get some sleep. You should do the same. There will be no rest. Tomorrow may be the day in which even the dead are reawakened."

Servius walked among the dead that night in the dark, lying in his cot. He could remember his childhood, before his mother died of fever. He could remember his father before he left for Rome the last time, and came home near death. By then, Servius had taken over running the estate. It had been a long, and difficult two years. Servius could remember his father telling him that if he had any sense, he would never turn to politics. Yet, here Servius was —an appointed Senator, and the joint commander of a military expedition to save the Emprire, or what was left of it.

Servius was unsure, uncertain, still. He felt cold once more, but not from the cold outside. There evil that awaited them beyond the next mountain. In the morning, the legion would be victorious, or they would all be dead. Servius breathed in deeply to settle himself, the knowledge that he himself might be dead, either in victory or in defeat, strong and powerful against his heart. Men would die tomorrow. Men of Rome leaving families behind. Even the fiercest barbarians would be missed by their own.

By organizing this legion, by calling for it, Servius wondered if, at the end of everything, God would hold him responsible for the deaths of those men. That, perhaps, was the most burdensome, terrifying thought of all. Servius could then only place his trust in Christ.

X

The morning dawned gray and cold, the sun a fiery, red orb along the horizon of the mountains, tall and silent sentinels in the northern winds. Where the clouds broke, a luminescent rose sky appeared. The weather had turned cold once more; much of the mud was frozen, covered with a thin veneer of ice. Snow still covered most of the land around the road through the pass, and blanketed the mountains and the hills.

At the very crest of the Aquilan Slope, behind the barricades for the archers, Scipio, in full battle armor, sat astride his horse. To his right was Servius, also in armor, and Titus and Horatio. To Scipio's left were Titinius and Modius; and behind them stood a small squadron of the mounted Emperor's Guards, to act as messengers and an escort. The main force of mounted Emperor's Guards waited just outside the village. On foot before Scipio stood Decinius, waiting for the first sign of enemy activity to go and join the ranks. The Legio Votum had taken its positions, shields, spears, and swords prepared. Men selected as archers waited behind the barricades, and fifty men waited in camp.

A number of the male villagers had assembled themselves outside of town, bearing what weapons they could —some of them donning their old uniforms if they had ever served —and offered themselves as reinforcements. Scipio had thanked them for their voluntarism, and placed them in as the last line of reserves —a kind way to both accept and deny their inclusion in combat, for which most of them would be utterly outmatched, presenting moving targets.

And Father Marcellus, his robes blown about by the wind, went along each rank, praying for the men, urging God to keep them safe.

On horseback now, through the pass ahead, rode two men —scouts sent ahead by Scipio to watch Rufus, returning at tremendous speed with tremendous urgency. Carefully moving their horses through the stakes and the pits, they passed through the formations, up to Scipio. The lead scout saluted.

"General," he reported, "Rufus is moving this way. Heavy weapons have been left in their place, but he's organizing every foot soldier in the camp it seems. He has a sizeable force of cavalry, that is taking the first position in line. But they're all coming this way."

"Very good," Scipio said. "Very good. Everything is in order."

In the distance, a handful of black-clad riders appeared, circling about, looking towards the slope, covered in Roman troops.

"Their scouts," Scipio said to Servius. "They know we're here, now. They will commit, or they will be forced back into Gaul. If they stay where they are, that gives us time to deploy the XIV Legion on its arrival, and then Rufus won't have a chance at all."

The Gothic scouts withdrew from sight, and silence fell across the mountain pass; the occasional cough, or a whinny from a horse, or the shifting of armor and shield, were all that could be heard.

And then, suddenly, there was a dull thud, a dull sound in the distance, a quiet rumbling, the coming storm. The thud grew louder, and was not thunder, but the sound of innumerable drums, a slow, singular, rhythmic beat. And up into view emerged the darkened figures of Rufus's Gothic confederation, his infantry, grouped but without ranks, form without order, a great, blackened mass creeping across the land.

The Romans looked at one another, drew deep breaths, steadied themselves as best they could; some of them men became sick, but straightened up; some made the sign of the cross; some shifted their weight from one leg to the other. Servius inhaled the cold, mountain air, steadied himself as best he could in the saddle.

The drumbeats grew louder, and echoed off the walls of the mountains around them. The Goth troops came to a halt, bearing all manner of weapons, from swords and small, round shields to clubs, daggers, and spears. Most of them sported wide, long beards, and wore large animal furs about them. Suddenly, they erupted into cheers, and passing among them on a great, black steed, riding up a small ledge, followed by a unit of bodyguards, passed Rufus himself, dressed exactly like his men—yet he wore no helmet, and wore a long, black cloak.

"But for an arrow that could be fired accurately over so great a distance," lamented Scipio.

Rufus raised his sword high over his head, shouting at his men, inspiring them to heroic acts of combat against their enemy, perched on the ridge, beneath a golden standard. The barbarians cheered raucously, and stepped back away to the edges of the pass, clearing an aisle between them.

Through the aisle then emerged their cavalry, bearded men on dark steeds, bearing spears, swords, and bows. They spread out to the width of the pass beyond their infantry, forming a ragged, but solid mass. Rufus yelled out something, his shrill voice high above the heads of his army, and the cavalry lunged forward in an all-out charge.

"This is it," Decinius said as he turned to head down the slope to the front lines.

The Goth cavalry surged on, kicking up mud and snow in their wake, screaming curses, screaming obscenities, yelling like monstrous creatures, spurring their horses on, faster. They swarmed toward the Aquilan Slope like hornets, driving on, driving forward, growing ever closer, ever nearer, perhaps two thousand men in strength.

Scipio raised his right fist. "Archers!" he called. "Prepare to fire a volley on my order, and then fire at will!"

The archers prepared their bows, raised them high, the arrows ready, the drawstrings taut, the Goth cavalry coming closer, coming closer all the while.

"Now!" Scipio shouted. "Fire!"

Three hundred arrows were loosed, soaring over the heads of the Roman troops below, and came slicing down through the Goth cavalry, tearing into horses, toppling riders, piercing skin and flesh; men went flying, horses reared and fell, tripping those behind amid cries of agony and the spurting of blood, yet the cavalry came on, even beneath the weight of successive volleys of arrows.

Servius watched in confused horror as the cavalry continued on, making no real attempt to avert the stakes, which pierced horse and man alike without effort, like a stone thrown through glass. Other horses skidded and reared, despite the urging of their masters, throwing riders off; others toppled headlong into the freshly-dug pits, and the sickening sound of breaking bones and armor against human bodies filled the air. The archers continued firing, raking down cavalry; the attack was halted, but the cavalry was not broken. The Goths raised their own bows then, to return fire; Roman troops in the ranks were hit and fell where they stood as shields were raised for protection.

The Gothic archers were accurate, and raised their bows even higher to the crest of the slope, loosing arrows that fell among the Roman archers, striking some, and even hitting a member of the Guard behind Scipio. The Guards moved forward at once with their shields to protect the commanders.

"Senator Servius!" called Scipio. "I order you to return to the camp!"

Servius said nothing at first, arm before him protectively against the Goth arrows.

"Now!" commanded Scipio. "Return to the camp immediately!"

Remembering Scipio's conditions, Servius reluctantly urged his horse back and away from the slope, followed closely by Titus and Horatio.

A strong wind swept down from the mountains, sweeping snow from the peaks across the pass. The Goth cavalry, disorganized and halted, began taking heavier losses as Scipio ordered the archers to double their action; one by one, the cavalrymen began to withdraw, began to fall back, until at last, the entire charge had sent reeling back, the Roman front lines untouched. Innumerable fur-covered corpses and the bodies of horses littered the ground.

Scipio called for the surgeon's team, and the wounded and the dead were picked up and removed from the lines, telling Titinius, "We have stung Rufus." Those injured that could still manage to carry a weapon were put in the back ranks. But from out in the pass now came the sound of a single horn —and the hordes of Goth infantry swept forward, with archers in the lead.

"And now," Scipio said, "we will contest for the high ground."

Servius rode into the encampment with Titus and Horatio; the men left to defend the camp, including the archery team from the Circus Maximus, asked about the progress of the battle, and Servius replied that the first Gothic attack —a cavalry charge —had been repulsed. From somewhere now emerged the sound of another drum, and at first, Servius believed that it might be the signal for the infantry attack on the slope. But the more he listened, the more unsure he was about where the sound was coming from.

Wordlessly, he urged his horse into a gallop toward the old mining path, with Titus and Horatio in pursuit.

"Sir! What are you doing?" called Titus.

"I need to be certain of something!" Servius shouted, heading into the pass, which descended at a gentle slope to a small plateau, and then descended into a narrow valley. The closer toward the plateau Servius came, the more and more he feared the source of the drum.

And there, below him, perhaps a mile out, winding its way through the dangerous turns and hairpin twists of the old mining pass, was a long, solid, body of black-uniformed troops, making slow but steady progress.

"Dear God," Servius said breathlessly. "They're going to flank us."

"Archers!" called Scipio, raising his sword aloft. "Prepare to fire!"

The swarms of Gothic warriors poured across the distance between themselves and the Romans in the main pass, banners held high and swords raised; their screams were wild and the hatred in their voices clear, ringing out through the sky. As they approached the bodies of the first of their cavalrymen on the ground, Scipio pulled down his sword.

"Fire at will!"

The Roman archers opened up on the Goths, raining arrows down on them; dozens of Goths fell to the ground; others, wounded only, continued on; still the advance came on, unfazed. The Roman archers continued firing, and the Goths came upon the stakes and pits at a dead run. Many, as the cavalry had before, met their fates against the stakes; others fell helplessly into the pits, unable to bring themselves to a stop.

Caught in a midst of confusion, the Gothic infantry faltered; but their archers opened fire on the Roman positions in greater numbers than the cavalry had, littering the slope with arrows and Roman bodies, causing the Roman archery fire to slacken. The Gothic commanders exhorted their men on, rallying them, and the black-uniformed barbarians began the ascent up Aquilan Slope in force, leaving their dead and dying brethren in their wake.

"Legio Votum!" shouted Scipio. "Prepare to defend this position! Prepare to meet the charge!"

Throughout the Roman ranks, commanders called for shields to be raised, and the spears put forward. Decinius raised his sword among his men, front and center.

"Men!" Decinius called. "Forward!"

The Roman groups moved forward in concert, spears leveled, their comrades at their backs with spears raised above their shoulders. The Goths came on like ocean water at the shore; and were within yards of the Roman troops.

At last, both sides met in a terrific clash of metal and armor; men screamed, were thrown up and back; spear pierced flesh; swords hacked apart limbs; blood poured out onto the muddy ground amid the broken beings, and the Roman ranks held, the Emperor's Guards at the fore.

"Keep your ranks!" shouted Decinius, urging reserve ranks to take the places of fallen men. "Keep it together!"

The Goths recoiled, stunned by the Roman advance, but regrouped quickly, and supported by reinforcements, recommitted to the attack. They surged upward, slicing and hacking at the Roman shields, hurling spears and firing arrows, swinging swords and using their own bodies at last against the Roman ranks, finally creating a break in the lines.

"Draw swords!" shouted Decinius. "Keep with your fellow men! Keep with your men!"

Scipio, watching from above, noticed the break. "Order the second groups forward at once!" he commanded. "We have to keep the lines together!"

"Yes sir!" said Titinius, saluting as he urged his horse down the slope.

"Modius!" said Scipio. "Bring forward the gladiators and the volunteers, and form them up just below the crest of the slope here!"

"Yes, sir!" said Modius, turning away toward the third line.

A wave of arrows came down on the crest of the hill, one striking a guard behind Scipio, and one skimming Scipio's arm. From the rear now emerged the auxiliary cohorts, moving quickly across the snowy, muddied ground as the second groups of Roman infantry moved down to join the Guards and the reserves already in combat.

"General Scipio!"

Scipio turned around, incredulous and incensed as Servius galloped toward him.

"What are you doing here!" Scipio demanded. "I ordered you to the camp!"

"Scipio! There are Goths coming up the mining pass! You have to send troops!"

Scipio shook his head. "It must be a scouting party!" he called. "We'll have time to deal with them later! I cannot spare a man, now! Get back to the camp! At once!"

There was no time to argue the point; Scipio was doing what Servius had hired him to do. Servius took off across the cold earth back to the encampment, reigning in the horse just beyond the anxious men there, waiting for news of the battle.

"They've committed their infantry," Servius said. "But we have another problem. We have Goths moving up through the pass here, in force. Gather what weapons you can. We're going to have to hold the old pass ourselves."

The men in the camp looked among each other, nervously, but Servius was undeterred.

"Make sure you bring plenty of arrows," he said. "Maybe we can stall the Goths long enough to either wait out the main attack, or to stop the flank assault. Let's go! Now!"

Instantly, the men rushed about, collecting bows and arrows from the wagons; many of the civilians from the town's volunteer unit came forward, offering to help, and Servius accepted it gladly. Among them was Felix.

"Room for one more?" he asked, picking up a bow.

"Glad to have you," Servius said.

"Sir," said Titus as the hastily-assembled group raced toward the plateau, "you ought to dismount!"

"No," said Servius, bringing his horse to a stop. "The men must see that I am not afraid, and the Goths must know there is someone to oppose them." Scipio glanced around him, imagining he had perhaps sixty or seventy men.

"Find good cover!" Servius ordered. "When they get in range, open fire, and don't stop for anything!

Make sure you keep your swords at hand, because if it comes down to it, we'll need them! Men from the Circus Maximus, move around and help those who have not fired a bow before, and do your best to keep firing as well."

Titus and Horatio then moved up alongside Servius, shields out and to either side of the senator.

"If you're not going to dismount," Horatio said, "you're going to remain here."

"Very well," said Servius. The Goths below them were closing in, a column nowhere near the size of the force in the main pass —but a column that could swat away Servius and his men like gnats.

"Keep together!" Decinius shouted, swinging his sword and felling a Gothic warrior. "Keep it together!"

The Roman lines had disintegrated; hand-to-hand combat ensued. This, Scipio knew, would be where the gladiators and the volunteers could be most effective: an all-out charge. He could see the Goth troops below; some of them were breaking and retreating —that meant that the Goths were near their end.

Scipio went forward before the last wave of Romans. "Men!" he shouted. "This is where we send them running back! For the glory of Rome, forward!"

The final Roman line let out a crushing cheer, and then raced headlong down the hill. Looking up and seeing the charge, many of the barbarians began to pull back; realizing their friends were behind them, and seeing their enemies fall away before them, the embattled Roman troops pressed on.

"Let's go!" Decinius called. "Let's go! Break them!"

"Open fire!" called Servius to the men around him, and a host of arrows arced skyward, and came falling down upon the Goths before them. Yet unlike the archers in the main pass, the inexperienced archers here were only half-effective. "Keep firing!" he called.

The Goths kept on their advance, moving steadily through the pass, reaching the foot of the plateau, stepping over the bodies of their fallen comrades. Their own archers opened up on Servius's position, and a dozen of his men went down. The Goths were within a few hundred yards.

"This is going to come down to the sword," said Titus.

"Horatio," said Servius. "Go to Scipio, now. See what is going on in the main pass, and tell him that if we will be overrun here if he does not send us reinforcements."

"Yes, sir!" agreed Horatio, urging his horse to a gallop.

"Keep firing, men!" shouted Servius, drawing his grandfather's sword. "Keep the pressure on them!"

Horatio arrived at the Aquilan Slope to see the Roman troops flowing down the incline, and forming up once more at the obstacles erected the day before; the Goths, shattered, were streaming back through the pass, and Rufus was nowhere to be seen.

Scipio stood triumphant at the crest, his guards arrayed around him.

"General!" Horatio said, riding before Scipio. "You have to head to the mining pass, now! Servius had deployed the camp guards there; the Goths are moving forward with a flank assault, in force!"

Scipio's face fell; his eyes displayed anger. "Impossible," he said. He looked down the hill. The legion would never be able to reform and make it in time to defend the old pass. There was only one possible option.

"Quick," he said. "To our own cavalry. We have once chance!"

With over half his men wounded by arrows, including Titus, Servius knew that their defense had come to an end. They would be forced to meet the Goths head on. The senator dismounted his horse, and put on his helmet. "Men!" he called. "Form up!"

Setting their bows aside, picking up their shields, and drawing their swords, the soldiers formed up in three ranks, with the civilian volunteers behind. Servius positioned himself in the first line, though he was without a shield. If anyone should die first, he thought, it should be him.

"Hold together, men," Servius said, his heart racing, and his stomach in knots. "Hold together, and we will hold them back."

The Goths were now only a hundred feet away, screaming, crying shrilly, the fearsome barbarian hordes moving closer, closer.

But then, up from their right flank, across the hill came the sound of a trumpet, and down from the woods poured the mounted Emperor's Guard, swords flashing in the sun, crashing with sheer fury and might into the side of the Gothic assault. The barbarians reeled, their momentum checked; and at the top of the hill to the right now appeared Scipio and Horatio.

The Emperor's Guard pushed forward, slashing and hacking their way through the enemy, giving those in front nowhere to run. The barbarians in the rear of the column broke, and began retreating back down the pass, pursued relentlessly by the Roman cavalrymen.

Rufus had been beaten back.

The screams of the wounded reverberated through the still night air. The Roman medical staff worked tirelessly, patching up injuries and performing amputations where needed. Many of the women from Colonia Aquilo also pitched in to tend the injured; and the men began to dig a hasty, mass grave.

Scipio met with Servius, a bloodied and bandaged Decinius, and Modius in the command tent. Titus stood nearby, the arrow that pierced his arm removed, and the wound already sewn and bandaged. Horatio stood beyond him.

"I have the figures," Modius said.

"Let me have them," the aged general said, sitting down.

"The auxiliary cohorts sustained 994 casualties, severely wounded and dead. The veterans, 144. The reserves, 654. The fit volunteers suffered 88. The cohort of gladiators, 106. And the Emperor's Guard suffered 417 casualties. Altogether, we lost 2,215 men today, just less than half our strength. We have 2,285 men alive or lightly injured. And we have confirmed that Titinius was indeed killed, along with seven of the villagers who volunteered to fight."

Scipio shook his head. "And any idea of the Goths?"

"At least five thousand, maybe six. We didn't have time to do an accurate count. We won't know until we've buried them all."

"We did better today than I'd anticipated," Scipio said. "Modius, Decinius... Go among the men with Father Marcellus. Let them know they performed splendidly this afternoon. And remind them of the importance of their sacrifices." Both officers saluted, and left the tent.

"Senator Servius," said the old general, noticing that the younger man was quiet and withdrawn. "Your little operation succeeded. And you saved Rome. I've sent scouts out. Rufus has completely withdrawn to his encampment, and there are no signs of movement. He won't attack again tomorrow. I wager that in a day's time, he'll have left the valley for Gaul. I've also sent two messengers out to bring word of our victory to Rome."

Scipio stood, and put his hands on the table before him. "You did a brave thing this afternoon, Servius. You slowed that diversionary attack long enough for me to send the cavalry. I should have sent them sooner."

"It doesn't matter, now," Servius said quietly.

"You were ready to die this afternoon," Scipio said. "That kind of courage is unmatched by almost everyone in that Senate. And now you're alive, and thousands are dead, and you've survived —and you're wondering why God spared you, and not another. No one can answer that, except God. The best we can do is understand that there is a reason for everything that happens. But I strongly suspect that you were spared because this was not meant to be your end; this is only the beginning of your story."

Scipio walked to the edge of the tent, and pulled back the flap. "Look around you," Scipio urged. "Thousands are dead, but thousands are still alive. The loss of life is not a beautiful thing, otherwise men would die by the millions. Life is worth preserving. And as you reminded me a few nights ago, saving Rome means saving millions."

Servius nodded.

"There will be countless more battlefields," Scipio said unhappily. "There will be countless more wars, and innumerable men will die, sometimes for the right reasons, sometimes for the wrong. War is not something men grow joyfully accustomed to in that they should enjoy destruction; and that is how it should be. War is an evil thing, but sometimes a necessary thing. And I think you understand that about today."

Servius nodded once more. "Yes."

Scipio knew the disheartened look in Servius's face, knew that Servius was like all other men and women who had lived to see such terror and times. Scipio himself had carried the same weight in his heart following his first battle –and it was a weight he carried still, though he hid it well for the sake of his troops.

"Well, then," Servius said. "I believe I will turn in. Wake me if there is news."

"It will be done," Scipio said.

But Servius did not go to sleep at once. Instead, he went through the battlefield, keeping his face stern, keeping his emotions in check, walking among the dead. He could see Father Marcellus moving among the dead as well, saying prayers, blessing the departed souls of the bodies for burial. He and Marcellus glanced at one another, nodded their respects, and went on. The cold had returned, and swept down, icy, from the north.

Ahead, Servius discovered Felix, his arm in a sling, with a woman and two girls beside him, coming forward.

"This is Senator Servius," Felix told his daughters. "He has saved our home."

Felix's wife dutifully bowed her head, and the two girls came forward with two aged, pressed flowers.

"We collected these in the late autumn," the older girl explained. "They grew wild on the slope. We put them between the pages of our Bible, and kept them to remind us of beauty even in the darkest times in winter. We want you to keep them, now."

Servius accepted the tender gifts, and Felix and his family went on. This beautiful, quiet town, at the center of a storm. Any town in the Empire. Any small town of dreamers, and families, and homes. A town of dreams... and dreamers... Moving away from the burial parties, and the soldiers and people moving around, Servius came to the side of one of the mining shacks. Putting his weight against his arm, and his arm against the wall, he inhaled and exhaled deeply, slowly, fighting the tears that formed at the corner of his eyes, but a single tear escaped, plummeting to the snowy ground below.

"God forgive me," he whispered.

XI

The new morning dawned clear and sunny and warm. The surviving members of the legion, though grounded by the reality of the previous day, and pained by the loss of their friends and, in some instances, brothers, fathers, or cousins —were nevertheless in as good a mood as possible. They knew they had driven back Rufus in battle, and the advance guard of the XIV Legion, with Valerus at the fore, had arrived in the valley behind them. Within a few hours, the entire legion would be there. Cheers went up when it was discovered that Rufus's camp had disappeared overnight, and the Goths were gone.

While Scipio was satisfied with the news, he was not totally convinced. He therefore organized patrols to head out every few hours, to observe where Rufus had camped, and to move on, to see if they could locate the Gothic army. Servius, Scipio noticed, though still subdued, was much improved from the previous evening, having come to accept what had happened as what had happened, and there being little else that could have been done. Wherever he went, the soldiers and the citizens of Colonia Aquilo smiled, waved, and congratulated him on the previous day's actions, and for fighting to raise the legion in the first place.

Servius found Scipio at the crest of the Aquilan Slope, the burial parties still at work removing corpses. Many of the bodies of the Goths were simply thrown into the pits near where they had died.

"We'd already dug their graves," Scipio said humorlessly. "We were outnumbered. Severely. Had this been a season other than winter, we would not have held."

"Why did we?"

"The snow and the mud, as I had predicted, slowed their advance. They used a lot of energy coming up from the valley, and charging from the start. In the warm spring, or the summer, or the autumn, there would be no snow, no mud to slow them down, no cold to sap their strength. By the time they reached our lines, they were out of breath; the stakes and the pits broke up their front. The fact that our men were in one position, were better rested, and better prepared for this fight meant that we won the day."

"That," the old general added, "and the fact that what moved their hearts to fight against the barbarians only fueled our determination."

"And what was that?" Servius asked.

Scipio smiled. "Hope."

Servius smiled as well. "How was it that you moved the cavalry over the mountain? I have been curious about that since yesterday."

"Your friend, Felix, told us about an old mining trail that went between the town and the old pass across the mountain. We used that."

"I will have to thank him," Servius acknowledged gratefully. "I suppose it's fine to criticize home until home must be defended."

"Or maybe," said Scipio, "you, and all of us, gave him some understanding of himself, of what Rome was always supposed to be."

"And will be again," Servius affirmed.
"What an enterprise this is," Scipio said in wonder. "An army of veterans, athletes, reserves, members of the Emperor's Guard, farmers and tradesmen, merchants and aristocrats and patricians... When I first set out, I had grave doubts I would even be alive to understand why we lost this fight. But I would not let those doubts get in the way of my mission. All of this tells me that Rome is far from finished. And for that... Servius, you will forever have my loyalty for this, for giving me this chance. I will continue to serve as long as I live."

"Thank you," Servius said. "If Rome is to survive, she'll need generals like you."
Cheers erupted from behind them, and both men turned to look back toward town, toward the encampment –and Valerus and his guard had arrived.

Valerus was awed and happy to learn the Goths had been thrown back by the new legion, but was equally disappointed he had not arrived in time. He was also profoundly impressed to learn that Servius had been the architect of the legion in the first place, and had been the reason Scipio had returned to command. Valerus, in his late thirties, had barely been back to Rome since he was sixteen, when he went off to join the army. It was the only thing he knew in life, he explained to Servius.

"And so how do we proceed now?" Valerus asked Scipio and Servius.

"We know Rufus is gone," said Scipio. "But the question is, where? I've sent out scouts to see where; it is possible that he has gone back to Gaul; or, perhaps, he has simply only gone to the next valley, worried we may strike him."

"As an expedition," Servius continued, "we were sent here to deal with Rufus. Until we know that he is no longer a threat, we must remain in the area. I have done much thinking this morning. Once we know that Rufus is gone, I will send word to the Senate in Rome that the XIV should be reassigned to this place, and our legion will be disbanded. I will also recommend that the northern central region of Italy be transformed into a new district, with new legions in addition to the XIV. And I will recommend Scipio to command the entire front."

"I'll have conditions," Scipio said with a laugh.

Three days later, in Rome, crowds filled the forum before the Senate curia. Majorian himself appeared before the people on the steps in the sunlight, members of his Guard, and of the Senate behind him. Orianus and Vespius looked on proudly. Wreaths and garland adorned the building; young girls threw flower petals up into the wind, and the citizens awaited the Emperor's official proclamation on the Legio Votum.

"A few days before," Majorian stated, "the Legion won a tremendous victory for Rome against Rufus."

The people cheered, throwing flowers and silk ribbons in the air. Among them were Prisca, and Amica; Prisca clutched Servius's cross in her hands, her breathing difficult.

"I have received word from Senator Servius himself that the legion is in good spirits, and that the XIV has joined them to make sure that Rufus will not pose such another threat."

The people cheered; and Prsica cried, a smile broadening across her face. Servius was alive.

"People of Rome," Emperor Majorian went on. "The Senate —your Senate —has voted to raise new, professional legions that will join the sides of those already serving, to preserve our Empire!"

The people continued cheering, chanting the name of the Emperor. But there were two who did not share in the celebration. Liberius and Cleander watched the forum, not from the curia, but from the roof of Cleander's second home.

"Let them cheer," Liberius spat. "Let them live. They have no idea of what powers await them." He turned to Cleander. "This is exactly what I was trying to avoid! A people inspired! A people with hope! Such a people will fight a new ruler, rather than accept him."

Cleander shook his head. "Rufus."

"Yes," said Liberius. "And I at the head of Rome as part of Rufus's empire. But now, this is getting out of hand. Romans dare to dream once more! Rome is finished."

"What will you do?" Cleander challenged him. "Numerius is dead. It is possible that Rufus never saw the message, or he would not have attacked Servius. Perhaps Rufus has broken his word to you."

"Nonsense! Rufus would not break his word to me, for he knows that Rome is still powerful enough to challenge him, and powerful enough to fight with him! Without Rome, his confederation and his plans of European conquest are impossible. I would imagine he mistook Numerius and his guards as an advance element of some sort, perhaps the head of a legion. But whatever the case is, Rufus has to move at once in order to cut this problem off at the head, before the new legions are raised and trained."

Liberius glared at the sight of jubilant celebration below him.

"Did you know that I am not a native of this city?" he asked Cleander.

"I did not."

"I was born and grew up on a villa near Colonia Aquilo," Liberius revealed. "It was I who gave Rufus the information about the pass, that it would be his best chance to take northern Italy, to head south and strike at Rome. Yesterday, after Servius's pitiful victory was unveiled in the curia, I sent word via three separate messengers to Rufus that the melting snow will give him no shortage of routes into northern Italy.

"One, in particular, I traveled as a child in the summer with my father on his business ventures in Gaul. It is the Augustan Way, an old road, narrow, timely to cover for an army of such size, but one that is safely ensconced by the mountains. It circles around for miles before coming out in the Aquilan Valley. It is impassable in winter, but should be passable now. They can take Servius and Scipio from behind, catching them by surprise, and putting them into the ground.

"And then there will be nothing to stop Rufus."

The soldiers encamped around Colonia Aquilo were in good spirits, and good order was prevalent. Children from the village ran about the tents, playing Roman and Barbarian; the soldiers of the XIV began constructing a lumber and earthen wall –a series of them –in the main pass, with the intent of stopping any potential future assaults by the Goths –or any enemy – from reaching the point of hand-to-hand combat. Even the old mining pass received three walls and a tower.

The wounded began to recover, while some of the more severely wounded passed on. The Legio Votum put to drills, to continue its interrupted training; and several of the men from the village volunteered to become active soldiers, and joined the Legion of Hope.

The XIV Legion, beyond its engineering skill, also brought a welcome sight to those living in the area. Heavy weapons, such as catapults, and other smaller weapons, such as various kinds of ballistas, capable of launching large, arrowlike projectiles, and flurries of smaller arrows at the enemy. Such weapons could greatly bring a battle to the favor of the Roman troops –and they gave confidence to the inexperienced members of the Legio Votum as well.

To Servius, at last, all of Rome might have been saved by the stand they made at Aquilo. It was possible, he knew, that the frontier troops may have been able to shift around to meet the threat at the last possible moment; and it was also possible that Rufus may have altogether abandoned his designs on Italy, at least temporarily. But these scenarios were unlikely, Servius knew. He could remember the refugees, streaming down from the mountains just two weeks before, and now, at least, there would be no more refugees for the moment.

Servius made his way over to the edge of town, to the church where Father Marcellus would be conducting an outdoor mass for anyone who wished to attend. There, soldier knelt beside civilian, heads bowed for the benediction thanking God for the victory of the previous morning.

"Now," said Orianus, circling the cellar of his house on the Palatine Hill. "Let's try this one more time. What on earth were you leaving Liberius's house for at such a late hour the other night? And what was it you threw into the river when you were accosted?"

Vespius sat against one of the walls, watching the man, tied to a chair, that Orianus stalked around. Several members of the Emperor's Guard waited upstairs.

"I have no idea what you're talking about," said the man. "I was merely returning home."

"A peasant returning to his home on the Palatine from Liberius's home? Ha! You've been in this cellar for two days, and you'll be here for two more or until you tell me why Liberius sent out messengers."

"This is most unbecoming of a senator!" the messenger said defiantly. "I'll report you to Liberius, to the Senate! You have no right to imprison a citizen of Rome!"

"Answer the questions, and I'll let you go," Orianus said.

"I have nothing to answer!" the messenger retorted.

"I've had Liberius's home under watch since the Legio Votum left Rome. And in all that time, three individuals have left his home at different times. You were the third. Now, I know that Liberius needs no household help, for he has more than enough slaves. His appetites are for women, not men. He is corrupt in broad daylight, so he has no reason to hide his senatorial misdoings by the darkness. So that begs the question: what are men doing leaving Liberius's home so late at night? Because I know you're messengers of some kind."

"Senator Servius would be appalled," the man said.

"Senator Servius," said Vespius rising, "is an moral idealist. We are not." Vespius reached into his robes, and pulled out a small purse of coins. "Judas betrayed our Lord and Savior for thirty pieces of silver. Perhaps you'll betray your devil of a master for double that."

The man's curiosity was then taken. "How much is in that purse?"

"Sixty pieces of silver," Vespius revealed.

"A message to Rufus," the man said suddenly.

Orianus stepped forward. "What message?"

"That Servius's troops are in the Aquilan Valley. That the old Augustan Pass can be used to come in behind them. Then there will be no opposition on his march to Rome."

"And why would Liberius send such a message?" seethed Orianus.

"He didn't say," said the man. "But Liberius told me I would receive an additional ten silver coins on my return in addition to the ten already given me."

"When was this message to be delivered?"

"As soon as I could find Rufus. The other messengers have a head start, so I was planning to take a ship north, so that I wouldn't have to waste time sleeping as I went."

Orianus turned to Vespius. "We have to get to the Emperor, and we have to send word to Servius at once." He then turned to the stairs. "Guards!"

The emperor's men came down, and Orianus gestured to the tied-up man.

"Bring him upstairs, and tie him up again to ride in the carriage."

"Wait!" shouted the messenger. "You told me you would let me go! You said that –"

"Gag him, too," commanded Orianus. "Quick, we don't have much time!"

Majorian was rousted from sleep beside his wife by his chamberlain, and wrapping himself in a robe, he stepped out of his rooms to find Vespius, Orianus, and scruffy-looking man, tied up, and held to the side by members of the Guard. Yellowed light from torches gave the hall in which they stood an almost ethereal quality, as if somehow the men present had stepped outside of time, or time itself had slowed to a stop.

"Speak," said Vespius, tearing the gag from the messenger's mouth.

When the man said nothing, Vespius smacked him across the back of his neck.

"Speak."

"Liberius sent out messages to Rufus, to tell him to use the Augustan Way to get in behind Servius and the XIV Legion. They'll have caught up with Rufus by now, and Rufus will have turned around."

"Captain," yelled Majorian to the leader of his personal bodyguard. "Put this man in prison and bring to me the fastest horsemen on the Palatine. Organize a detail to arrest Liberius at once."

"Wait!" said Orianus. "Don't do that yet, don't arrest Liberius. We don't know how many senators are with him, and we certainly don't want to cause a panic in the city. The people would turn into a mob if word of this gets out —and you know Liberius will see to it that it does. Wait on the arrest. I have Liberius's house under surveillance in case he makes any other moves."

Majorian growled. "What then?"

"We hope to God our messengers get to Servius in time. And for now, have your master of all forces, Ricimer, begin raising the new legions. The legislation passed gives power for these five new legions to be raised in April, but I'll put forward the amendment that changes the starting date to tomorrow. When pressed for why, I'll explain that the shifting of the XIV Legion to the Alps will mean that there will be friction sooner, rather than later, on the western line. I doubt that there will be many dissenting votes, if any at all."

"And when the situation is stable, I will have Liberius arrested and tried," said Majorian. "And executed."

"It is possible," said Vespius, "that the people may do it themselves."

In the church's adjoining hall —which served as a community gathering place for all manners of celebrations and gatherings —Servius held a meeting with the people of Colonia Aquilo. Parchment paper, ink, and stylus to at hand, Servius was determined to use his time away from Rome to continue speaking with people, seeking out their concerns, their suggestions, and their ideas. Felix, upon the opening of the meeting, remarked laconically that it was the first time a Roman senator had ever stepped foot in their village, let alone going to the people willingly to see what they had to say.

"I take that as a compliment," Servius said with humor and grace, causing the people in attendance to laugh.

As he expected, the first question asked by a miner had to with the military presence.

"Will a military outpost be maintained here?" the man asked. "Or will the legions be returned to the Alps? We've been living under threat of invasion for weeks... And with the Gallic uprising... We're up here in the mountains, just about defenseless. Why hasn't Rome raised more legions?" The people around him voiced their support of his question, and the man returned to his seat.

Servius finished taking notes on what the man had said, and then addressed the room.

"When the treasury becomes constrained," Servius said, "the Senate often targets the military, confusing the presence of stability with peace, rather than security being continually maintained by troops. And legions are, themselves, expensive to raise and maintain. But that is a cheap way to attempt to balance the books —and besides, the money will only be used elsewhere.

"I'm sorry that you've been without security here for so long. It is something that I believe will soon be changed. The presence of Rufus, and the victory we had yesterday, will confirm in the minds of the Senate the fact that we do need troops on the northern frontier. I do know for a fact that Emperor Majorian agrees with you: he wants troops up here on the frontier, and we have allocated funding for new legions. So I really do believe that it's only a matter of time before legions garrison themselves here permanently."

"Senator," said a woman, standing. "Would those legions ever be used to conquer lost territory? I mean, there are loyal Roman allies who seek our help. And now they're at the mercy of the Goths and the Gallic civil war."

"I can't say what the Emperor intends to do, but I can tell you that I favor supporting our friends and allies in every way that we can, including to reclaim lost territory. But if that is going to happen, our allies are going to have to pitch in, too. And I know that they will when the time comes." Servius watched as Felix shook his head, but he declined to say anything.

A farmer stood next. "Sir," he said; "We have been greatly impacted by refugees, and our food stores are low. Our crops have been exhausted, and the money we've voluntarily spent to assist those in need has left us seriously shortchanged. Will the Senate extend to us the three-fifth tax deductions granted to other regions impacted by invasions, as was done in the past?"

Servius made a note. "I'll certainly press for tax reductions in this region," he said. "There have been five villages razed; people can't pay taxes if they can't afford to take care of themselves."

Decinius and Scipio, watching from their seats in the back of the room, nodded to one another.

"I once told Servius that I would sooner stare down a barbarian horde than contend with the Senate," Scipio whispered.

"Has your opinion changed?" Decinius asked, favoring his bandaged arm.

"Yes," said Scipio. "I would sooner face down the Senate as a dishonest politician, than see what moves the hearts of regular people as an honest one. I would not want to let those people down. It's one thing for a senator to blame a soldier, for a politician to tell you what you're doing wrong, because most of the time, the politician is wrong and everyone knows it. But it's entirely something else to be confronted by a child, by a mother, or by a father, and have them tell you that everything you've done is wrong."

Decinius concurred. "I thought that, when I got older, I would try for the Senate. Now I think I'll try my hand at farming, and living quietly. Certainly I'll pay attention to what happens, and I'll make my voice heard —but to be in a position where you have to make such promises…"

"I agree," Scipio said. "Even when you can't follow through on something, even when you may be the only senator against hundreds, even when your failure is because things were completely out of your hands, and you still have to go back and tell the people you failed them… And there is a difference between something genuinely beyond your control, and throwing blame around to make yourself look better, to make yourself look like a victim, to make yourself seem innocent. An honest man takes responsibility."

Both men turned their attention back to Servius, who was scratching more notes onto his papers.

"I'll make sure the Senate is aware of the effects of the grain tariffs," he said. "Homegrown grain would be more cost-effective, and beneficial to the local economy, to Italy at large," he said. "Trade matters, but if we can keep prices down here by expanding our grain markets and lowering export tariffs, then we should."

"Ten days," Modius said as he surveyed the Aquilan Pass from the slope's guard tower. Scipio leaned against one of the walls of the tower while Valerus studied the new walls; Servius stood, his arms folded, his eyes on the horizon. "Ten days since Rufus disappeared. Our scouts haven't found him, all the nearby passes are clear... I think it's probably safe to say he's returned to Gaul to lick his wounds."

"Nevertheless, keep the patrols going out," said Scipio. "We want to make absolutely certain that Rufus isn't coming back."

"And if he does," Valerus said. "We'll be ready for him here."

A warm spring breeze echoed across the plateau, and the sun shone down and stirred to life the first flowers in the meadow, and the mountain farmers put their hands to the earth of their fields. Somewhere on the wind were the songs of birds; the snow, melting, withdrew from the land as though waves on the sand. The winter had ended.

Servius met again with citizens of Colonia Aquilo, citizens whom he had not yet met with. The doors to the meeting hall and church were left open, to allow in the beautiful wind. Just as the questions turned to tariffs, Titus appeared at the door.

"Senator Servius," he said, catching his breath. "General Scipio needs to see you immediately."

Servius excused himself, and exited the hall quickly, following Scipio across the soft ground. Across the way, both legions were bringing their numbers together; the men were beginning to bring down tents and pack up the wagons. Servius's own tent was being disassembled, overseen by Horatio.

"What's going on?" Servius asked, finding Scipio, who had just given orders to Modius and Decinius. Valerus had already gone off to his troops.

"We're moving out at once," said Scipio. "I received word from the Emperor this morning that our friend, Liberius, has betrayed us by giving Rufus another pass to take. Liberius has been in league with Rufus for God knows how long, and Rufus has appeared in the valley behind us, heading south to Rome. We're going to catch up to him, and attack him from behind. With all luck, by tonight, we'll put Rufus's head on a pike. Get your armor on, and prepare to move out. Father Marcellus will remain here until after the battle."

"Right," said Servius. "Right."

"And Servius," Scipio called after him. "This all ends today."

XII

Within three-quarters of an hour, the XIV Legion and the Legion of Hope were moving down through the Aquilan Valley, back the way they had come only days before. Combined, they amounted to more than 7,000 men. The heavy weapons, partially disassembled, were loaded onto wagons and brought along by teams of horses, while the infantry made up most of the column. The mounted Emperor's Guards move along the flanks of the little army, and rode ahead to see about Rufus's positions.

The men moved out in good order, making good time. The XIV led the way; the Legio Votum brought up the rear, along with the catapults and ballistae. An hour before noon, the column was well into the Aquilan Valley, approaching the extended pass Liberius had betrayed them with; signs of the movement of the Goths were visible. Muddy, churned earth in the form of footprint and horse hoof, as well as deep ruts from wagons and carts had turned a large swath of the valley countryside into a deep, hideous scar, leaving no mystery about the direction they had gone.

The advance scouts came pouring back to Scipio, at the head of the entire column with Servius and Valerus, the banners and legions of Rome resplendent in the late morning sun behind them.

"Sir," reported one of the scouts. "Rufus is ahead of us by an hour or two; it appears as if they're setting up camp."

"What on earth would they be doing that for?" Servius said.

"Either because they're expecting to stand and fight, or because they're not expecting us at all," said Scipio. He turned to the messenger. "Did you run into any of their riders? Any of their scouts?"

"No, sir," said the Roman scout. "They've begun setting up their camp on the other side of a ridge. You can see it from the next ridge over."

"And no one saw you?"

"No, sir, no one challenged us at all."

"Good. Head back out and keep an eye on them. Report any changes to me at once."

"Yes sir," saluted the scout and went off.

"We're going to keep moving faster," Scipio announced to Valerus and Servius, speaking the plan as it formed in his mind. "We'll draw up behind the second ridge and form up, then move the catapults onto the second ridge and invite Rufus to come at us. We'll position the Legio Votum at the fore, to give Rufus the image that that is all we have; when he commits himself, we'll commit the XIV Legion, and drive Rufus into his camp. We'll send the mounted units of both our legions around to the flanks, to act as a screen against their cavalry, and to cut through the Goths as they retreat. "They'll have nowhere to go, because we'll have cut their way back north off from them."

"The new legions are going to be raised in Terni," said Majorian as Orianuas and Vespius watched the Emperor's Guard prepare a caravan of wagons and horses outside the palace. "I'll be gone for a week, and will be conducting all official business through correspondence. I would prefer not to go, but Ricimer is overseeing the western front at the moment, and there is no one else I can trust enough to see that these new legions get off the ground in a quick fashion. There are too many bureaucrats that would delay things. If I'm present, there won't be any such obfuscation."
Majorian mounted his horse. "Keep an eye on Liberius and Cleander. Act as you see fit to keep them in check. If there is any emergency, do not hesitate to send for me, and I shall return at once. And as soon as you know what is going on with Servius and Scipio, let me know immediately, even if you have to bring the news yourself."

"We'll do so," said Orianus.

"Good," Majorian said. "With success, we'll be able to return the capital of the empire to Rome, permanently, I hope. If we can break this invasion, perhaps those wary about Rome will have their fears dissuaded."

With that, the Emperor and his Guard went off down the Palatine, their horses thundering across the cobbled streets, dust rising in their wake. As they passed the homes and residences of patricians and senators, anyone present cheered Majorian as he went past.

"The problem now," Orianus mulled out loud, "is that with the Emperor gone, Liberius will stretch his legs and extend his grasp. He was humiliated at Aurelian Field. He's looking to soothe his image, reclaim his power, and seek revenge against all of his enemies. Servius tops the list."

"Then we cannot fail him," said Vespius. "Majorian will be remembered as a capable emperor, and he is the right man to run the empire. But if Liberius succeeds, Majorian is deposed, and the Empire comes under the control of Rufus, then you and I are finished, too."

By early afternoon, the Roman column had come upon the ridge-laden eastern Aurelian Valley, and Servius could see Rufus's camp, right where the scouts had said it would be. Scipio quickly directed the troops into positions below the closer of the two rises, and the catapults were reconstructed. Scipio sent out scouts once more in all directions, to make sure there was no Goth cavalry on their flanks.

"Once we make our appearance at the top of this ridge," Scipio announced to Servius as he extended his hand up to point at the apex of the land, "Rufus will know for sure we are here, and there is no turning back." Modius and Decinius looked on.

Valerus appeared a moment later, his face confident and determined. "We're all ready," he declared.

"Very well," said Scipio. "Modius, Decinius... To your men."

Both officers saluted, and moved out to their troops. The catapults were secured to their horse teams; the battered Legio Votum drew its positions; the XIV Legion fell in rank behind them. Teams of soldiers prepared to carry the ballistae up the hillside.

Scipio has slightly altered his plans for combat. While the Legio Votum would appear on the hilltop, along with the catapults and ballistae, their formations by cohort would be interspaced, so that they could withdraw as the XIV Legion moved up. That way, the Legio Votum, which had suffered so dearly just days before, would offer reserves to the line instead of bearing the brunt of the coming charge. The XIV, upon advancing through the gaps of the Legio Votum, would then solidify their lines under the cover of their heavy weapons.

"Men!" Scipio said, riding along the lines of troops, his sword held high. "To the top! March!"

The sound of drums from the XIV Legion beat the advance, and with Decinius and Modius in the lead, the Legion of Hope stepped forward, and began the ascent. Scipio, Servius, Titus, Hortio, and Scipio's guards followed suit. The catapults and the ballistae were put into place. As Scipio and Servius crested the ridge, they could see the entire Gothic camp across the next ridge.

The enemy response was almost instantaneous. The two thousand men on the ridge could not be missed, and at once, the Goths were scrambling through their camps, picking up weapons, organizing in their amorphous formations. Drums and horns rang out among the tents and campfires; and a group of mounted men rode through, shouting orders.

"Probably Rufus," Scipio commented. "It looks as though they have a few thousand men among them. We may just outnumber them."

Yet, to Servius, something was not right. He scanned the camp, watching the Goths assume their battle lines, preparing to move forward, groups of hundreds and hundreds of men, their black garb a dark stain on the pastel green land.

"Where is their cavalry?" Servius wondered aloud as the Goths began their advance.

"Most of it was probably destroyed at Aquilo," offered a guard from behind.

"Not all of it," Servius said. "This is wrong. Something is wrong."

Scipio raised himself up in his saddle, looking around as the catapults opened fire. "If they're going to hit our flanks," he said, "our cavalry will delay them until we can shift units to deal with the threat."

Another guard spoke up from behind. "They're not going to hit our flanks," he said. "They're going to take us from the rear."

The entire command turned. Behind them, from the direction of the Augustan Pass, a long train of Goth cavalry was racing out across the fields.

"They're surrounding us," Servius realized aloud.

Scipio breathed in deeply, then shouted to his guards. "Get Decinius, Modius, and Valerus to me at once! Pull the auxiliaries and the volunteers from the ridge, and replace them with cohorts of the XIV! Put them into line with the XIV, and have the rest of the XIV take up positions halfway up this ridge! And have our cavalry withdrawn from our wings. We're going to need every man we can get."

Within moments, the entire Roman position was being changed; troops rushed forward, taking up new positions; the Roman cavalry began its return; and the ballistae opened fire on the Goth infantry, which had come in range.

Valerus arrived, followed shortly thereafter by Decinius and Modius.

"Snakes," Valerus said, watching the Goth cavalry continuing to close the circle around them. "This is going to be tough to handle."

"How did they get around behind us," Decinius asked.

"They must have kept their cavalry up the Augustan Pass," Modius spat. "And then came down behind us, following us."

"I should have sent patrols up that way," Scipio said, cursing. "This is my doing. And my doing to get us out of this."

"No one could have known," Valerus said.

"I should have known," Scipio cursed again.

"Their cavalry is closing a vise around us. There's precious little time to get out, Servius."

Servius looked at Scipio. "What?"

"I'm ordered you to leave," he said. "Head south to Rome. Tell them what has happened here."

"No," Servius said. "I'm part of this enterprise."

"There were conditions when I accepted command," Scipio said. "I admire your bravery but I expect you to obey my orders. You, Titus, and Horatio will return to Rome to raise the alarm. That isn't a request, it is an order."

"I respectfully refuse," Servius said, understanding that to remain would mean his death at the hands of the Goths.

"Senator Servius! Are you disobeying my order?"

"I am," said Servius.

"Good," Scipio said succinctly. "Then you're under arrest. Titus, Horatio, take this man back to Rome and do not release him from your custody until he is there."

Titus and Horatio reluctantly moved forward to either side of Servius.

"It's time to go, sir," said Titus.

"I'll throw you over my horse if I have to," Horatio said. "Respectfully, of course."

Servius breathed in deeply.

"There's no time to think," Titus said.

"Scipio," Servius said, gripped by humiliation and anguish. "I'll see you after all this is over."

With that, Servius and his two guards set out along the lines, racing out into the field beyond the legions, beyond the grasp of the Goth cavalry, and stole away toward the hills in the distance.

The Gothic infantry formations were ascending the slop of the first ridge, and paused there, waiting for their cavalry to close the circle around the entrapped legions. The catapults continued firing, as did the ballistae; several of the machines were turned, so that they could fire at the Gothic cavalry.

Scipio knew what must be done. There would be no elaborate tactics, no fortifications, no disciplined formations when it came down to it. This would be do-or-die, one man against another. The soldiers would fight with their backs to one another as long as they could, but in the end, it would come down to one against another, one Roman against one barbarian.

The Roman lines were brought in a circle, and Scipio urged his horse over to where the standard bearer of the Legio Votum stood with the standard guards. Scipio took the standard, and with it in his arm, rode before the ranks of men.

"Romans!" he shouted. "Romans, hear me now! The Goths are surrounding us, are preparing to charge. We cannot retreat, we cannot remove ourselves. Here is where we shall make our stand! This spot of ground you occupy is no longer northern Italy, but it is *Rome herself!* If the Goths move on, there will be nothing to stop them from taking all of Italy! So here, today, we defend all of the Empire!" As he spoke these words, he rode back through the cohorts.

There, he took the standard, and thrust it into the ground so that it stood on its own, facing north.

"We will defend our home!" Scipio cried. "We will defend this land! We will defend the last standard between us and Rome with our very lives! We will not fail!"

The legions raised their shields and spears in roaring affirmation, the chant of "Rome! Rome! Rome!" pouring from their hearts through their mouths.

It was a cheer that Servius, ascending to the crest of a nearby hill, heard as he stopped his horse to watch the valley below him. Titus and Horatio reigned in their horses, hesitant to stop, determined to get the young senator to safety, worried that the Goth cavalry would follow them. But Servius waited, watched the land below, watched the Goths close the trap.

"Remember to keep tight," Modius said, moving among the lines toward Scipio. "Keep your formations, keep your friends to your side and make sure you have your fellow's back."

"They've sealed us up," Scipio said, his breath short, the anticipation strong.

All at once, a single horn blared, and the black lines swept forward across the ground, running at full speed toward the crimson-uniformed Roman troops. The ground shook from the fury of thousands of feet pounding the earth; a sickening cry from the hordes rose up, unparalleled from the mountains. The Goth infantry surged across the first ridge, and swarmed before the Roman lines. They were out for blood.

Scipio watched the enemy cavalry galloping toward them, knowing that the cavalry could shatter their ranks and cause chaos. There was only one option to stop them, only one, singular, suicidal option to break up the charge and buy the infantry time.

That was itself a charge.

The catapults continued firing, and Scipio rallied to his side the five hundred men that were mounted, between the XIV Legion and the Emperor's Guard. It was not a charge that he would order someone else to lead; it was a charge that he himself would bring forward.

The Roman infantry opened a gap in their lines through which their cavalry passed. The cavalry quickly arrayed itself in two ranks, and readied their swords.

"For Rome!" shouted Scipio. "Charge!"

The Roman cavalry leapt to the attack, nearly flying across the open ground, trampling spring flowers and tearing apart the earth beneath. Their pennants whipped madly from the speed of the assault, and the riders let out a tremendous yell as they went hurtling toward the Goths.

In one single, explosive instant, the cavalry collided. The force of the thrust tore a gap in the Goth attack, causing the entire formation to fold and falter. Men were flung dozens of feet from their horses, only to be crushed to death underfoot; swords clanged as riders engaged one another, swinging and hacking at the closest enemy; horses reared and screamed in fright while men leapt from one mount to the next to topple their opponents. The Roman cavalrymen found their friends, defending one another from successive sword thrusts, but whatever the skill they had, they were utterly outnumbered.

"Fight on, men!" Scipio shouted, plunging his sword through the throat of an opponent, then swinging the sword above his horse, cutting down another Goth rider. "Keep the pressure on them!"

Back on the ridge, the XIV legion braced for the onslaught of the Goth infantry. They came rushing up the hill, throwing their weight against the Roman shields; the Roman lines held and the spears were pushed forward, skewering the enemy; but for each Goth that fell, another took his place, growling, screaming, swords swung down, clubs thrown forward, and the Roman line contracted, and reserves were put in.

Decinius himself plugged a hole in the Roman line, urging his men to fight, urging them to keep to their weapons. Decinius brought down one barbarian by slicing apart his arm, and then another by slashing open his unprotected ribs. A third came forward, pulling a sword down on Decinius's head, but Decinius blocked the move with the sword in his right hand, and pulled a dagger from his belt to thrust through the man's heart. A fourth Goth moved on, wielding a spear, which Decinius cut apart –but as he did so, he left his torso exposed – and a fifth Goth took the opportunity to plunge his sword into Decinius's side. The Roman commander reeled and recovered, pulling his sword down on the Goth's skull, splitting it. But the fourth Goth returned with his own sword, and pierced Decinius's heart, leaving him dead on the ground. But then there was another Roman soldier, slaying Decinius's killer, and taking his place in line.

Scipio's attacking force was dwindling quickly. Roman men fell left and right, fighting with their last breath, their last ounce of strength, the last beats of their heart. While some of the Goth cavalry had continued the assault on the Roman infantry, most of it had consumed the space around Scipio's charge.

The old general sliced open the chest of a Goth warrior as he attempted to lunge at him, and then severed another's arm as he reached to snatch away the reigns of Scipio's horse. But then he felt a sharp, terrible pain in his lower left side: a Gothic rider, unhorsed, had plunged a spear into Scipio, who in turn cut into the man's throat and shoulder, felling him. Attempting to remove the spear, Scipio was struck by an arrow that skimmed his upper left arm, but passed on. He brought his horse around, cutting apart the Gothic archer who had fired the arrow –but also to be slammed by the length of a spear, toppling him from his horse, and disappearing from sight.

The Goth cavalry pressed on, and overwhelmed the Romans.

Valerus watched from his position among the rear line of the legions as the main body of Goth cavalry tore down the field upon them. Ballistae opened fire on the horses, toppling dozens, but on the Goths came, faster, driven on by hatred and fury. "Prepare to meet the charge!" Valerus called.

Cohorts of the Roman XIV stationed along the rear lines moved into defensive positions, raising and barring themselves behind shields while extending spears forward. The cavalry came on, a flowing, unrelenting, unstoppable mass. With terrible force they slammed into the Roman formations, breaking it in some places, but being broken themselves in others. Yet it was enough: the Roman lines strained, and constricted, and the Goth infantry pushed forward, gaining a foothold on the crest of the ridge.

Servius, Titus, and Horatio watched it all, saw the breakthrough that followed, saw the collapse of the Roman position.

"Now, sir," said Titus. "We need to go."

Servius reluctantly turned his horse south, for the ride to Rome.

XIII

The city loomed large in the distance, cold and dark, quiet, settled against the early morning sky, still mostly dark, with a touch of deep blue on the horizon. Servius, Titus, and Horatio moved along at a trot, the ground difficult to see, but speed a matter of urgency. They passed into the city, past curious guards, and those on their way to the fields, to begin work at first light. But they were also seen by one of Liberius's hired thugs, who made haste to awaken his master.

"Do not kill them," Liberius ordered harshly. "You know the plans."

Loud rapping on the front door of Vespius's home thirty minutes later, just as the sun was rising, revealed four men who overpowered the answering servant, and swept to Vespius's room. There, they barricaded the door, locking an angry Vespius inside, and began to tear through the house, giving the impression of a robbery.

Orianus, having already awakened, was preparing to head to the market when the knock on his door came. Answering it, four thugs rushed in, but Orianus responded quickly, pulling out of his robes his stylus, and stabbing the first through the throat. The second lunged at Orianus, and Orianus grabbed his head, twisting it sharply, the sound of cracking bone following suit. The third found himself punched in the face, and the fourth leapt at Orianus, catching him by the midsection and forcing him down. The third man, recovered, grasped Orianus as well, and the two thugs dragged Orianus back to his room, pushing him inside, knocking him to the floor, and bloodying his head in the process. They then barricaded the door with an overturned case of shelves.

Prisca and Amica were already working in the kitchen, preparing food for the rest of the staff, when the pounding knock came at the door. But before either one could answer, the door was kicked in.

"Prsica," Amica said, pointing to the back window. "Go find Orianus or Vespius! Get out of here, quickly!" There was the sound of something being overturned in the courtyard. "They must be here for Servius! Get out! Quick!"

Prisca grabbed a rolling pin, and pulled herself through the window, dropping into the alley behind the house. But to her right appeared a brutish, bearded thug, who grabbed her arm before she could turn to flee. He then attempted to subdue her by taking her other arm, but she responded by swinging her foot up between his legs, causing him to relinquish his grasp in a deafening screech. She then brought the rolling pin down on his head, knocking him to the road, unconscious. Looking about, Prisca then raced down the alley, out onto the street, and over to Orianus's house.

There, she saw the door to Orianus's home was being watched by another thug, and she cut down the alley to sneak around behind to the next road, to Vespius's house. But before she go any further, she heard her name called. Looking back, she saw Orianus, his forehead bleeding, holding on with all of his strength to the window sill inside.

"Prisca," he said breathily. "Go to Terni. Tell the Emperor to come back at once. Tell him who you are, what has happened." He threw his signet ring to the ground. "Take my seal. It will get you to see him."

Prisca snatched up the signet and ran to the stable beside Orianus's house. There, she took Orianus's horse, and urged it down the Palatine Hill.

Servius and his guards, meanwhile, arrived at the palace, and Servius nearly jumped from his horse. He raced up the front steps, only to be confronted by Liberius and a host of hired men. Titus and Horatio appeared at Servius's side a moment later, swords drawn.

"Looking for someone?" Liberius asked in a mock tone. "The Emperor is in Terni, overseeing his new legions. But no worry, for I am here. But where is your legion? Where is your proud and capable Scipio? Nowhere? Did he meet with misfortune on the battlefield? Was your legion wiped out? Did you run away like a frightened dog? You coward."

Liberius's words were venomous. He snapped his fingers, and the thugs rushed around the three men, surrounding them.

"Senator Servius," Liberius said in a drawling voice. "I am placing you under arrest for desertion."

Titus raised his sword. "That's a lie!"

"Arrest them all," said Liberius. "Now."

"Senators," said Liberius as he took the floor before the empty throne in the curia. "I have called this emergency session in the Emperor's absence because I come before you today with a matter of the gravest and greatest importance, one which must be settled now. The Legion of Hope, and the XIV Legion, have been massacred by Rufus's confederation.

"Thousands of lives lost!" Liberius excoriated as the Senators talked among themselves, returning their attention to the floor. "Thousands of lives lost unnecessarily! We could have tried diplomacy! We could have tried peaceful measures! We could have attempted another try to talk to Rufus! But the warmongering of some —like Orianus and Vespius —have led us to the hour of death! And look around you! Those two criminals don't even have the courage or the decency or the respect to attend a meeting of this body!"

The room was silent. The seats usually occupied by Servius, Vespius, and Orianus were suddenly conspicuous, glaring. Their allies shifted in their places uncomfortably, realizing that Liberius now held the balance of power. Cleander grinned in his station.

"Speaking of courage," Liberius went on, "it is a virtue that Aristotle praised in his rule o the golden mean. But the deficiency of courage is cowardice. Bring him in!"

From the doors at the back of the room emerged two of Liberius's men, pushing forward a bound and gagged Servius, forcing him onto his knees in the middle of the curia. Some of the Senators began shouting.

"This is an outrage!"
"No Senator is to be treated this way!"

"Horrific!"

"Silence!" called Liberius. "Hear what I have to say, Senators! Hear me, now! Two days ago, the legions were massacred! Legions that Servius called on to be used, legions that Servius was given command of! It seems patently simple to me what has happened! Servius fled from his legion to avoid death! He ran away like a child!"

The curia exploded in raucous voice and chaotic shouting. Servius breathed in deeply, angry, struggling to free himself, unable to do so. Anger, humiliation, downfall.

"The only sentence for desertion," Liberius declared, "is execution!"

The Senators continued shouting, continued arguing, standing, moving around, waving their arms, pointing, their faces red, spittle flying from their mouths. Some called to kill Servius at once, while others demanded Servius be exiled, while others protested that Servius had not had a say, that he could perhaps be a survivor rather than a deserter.

And here, thought Servius, they argue about me when at this moment, the Goths approach.

Yet it was not the Goths who flung open the doors to the curia, catching all within by surprise. There, in the broad morning light the streamed onto the floor, stood Scipio and a handful of men, who threw down the thugs that had guarded the Senate. Scipio was bloodied, bandages about his arm, his cape shredded and torn, the Emperor's Guards with him battered and bruised.

Liberius was speechless, and a host of his hired minions lined up behind him.

"Senator," Scipio said in exhaustion. "I arrived in just an hour ago. I went to see the Emperor, to find out that he had gone to Terni. So I went to see Senator Servius, to find his home ransacked and he himself taken prisoner. I don't know what you think you're doing, but I—"

"*Seize them!*" shouted Liberious, recovering quickly. "They are here to overthrow the Senate! Arrest any man who sides with the traitors!"

Liberius's men rushed forward, and Scipio and his men raised their swords. A handful of thugs were cut down before they overwhelmed Scipio.

"A trial!" shouted Capito above the stunned Senate. "Give them a *public trial!* It is the *Roman way!*"

"Military deserters are executed summarily," Liberius returned.

"He is a Senator!" shouted someone else.

"A public trial!" shouted another.

"Very well," Liberius growled, understanding his hold on power was tentative. He had to retain as much control as he could, before the arrival of Rufus. "If you want a public trial, we shall try them all. Tomorrow at ten. Prepare the forum."

Prisca arrived on the outskirts of the town of Fara around dusk, thirty miles from Rome, barely holding on to the horse, sleep tugging at her. It wasn't difficult to find the encampments for the legions being raised, but locating Emperor Majorian would be something entirely different. At first, she tried the road along the camps, seeking the emperor's banners or his personal guard, but she was unsuccessful. She tried asking some of the military officers and volunteers, but none of them knew where the emperor was. A peasant farmer, on his way home from the fields, suggested Prisca try the town itself.

It was in town that Prisca found the emperor at the urban residence of a local patrician. The Guard was arrayed around the building, and the emperor's banners displayed proudly by the owner of the home. Prisca nearly fell from her horse, rushing toward the doors, with soldiers waving for her to halt.

"I have to see the Emperor," she said. "I carry the seal of Senator Orianus. This is an emergency!"

"Come with me," said one of the soldiers, bringing her into the home, and to the courtyard where Emperor Majorian was going over muster sheets.

"Emperor," said the Guard, saluting. "This young woman is here to see you. She bears the signet of Senator Orianus."

Majorian rose from his table, realizing at once that something was wrong. "You can tell me about it on the way," said the Emperor to Prisca. "Men! Bring up my carriage! Ready the horses! We ride to Rome!"

Servius sat with his head against the cement wall of the jail cell in the imperial prison, the shadows long, torch light flickering from the passageway beyond the bars. He closed his eyes, inhaling slowly, exhaling slowly, his arms folded, anxious. Scipio sat against the opposite wall, calmly observing the young man before him.

"I have to say," Scipio said, "you're taking this all quite well."

Servius opened his eyes, and looked at the aged general.

"I never even imagined this would happen," Servius said. "I'm sorry that you've been subjected to this... I just... I don't understand..."

"When I was imprisoned a few years ago, there was another young senator in prison as well. He had said something about Emperor Avitus that Avitus didn't like. I don't remember the offense, or the supposed offense. But this young senator, about your age, screamed and cried and attempted to break through the cell door. Life is precious, but so is dignity. That man had none. Here, you face death, and you're apologizing to me. You're a remarkable man, Servius."

Servius looked over as Scipio. "Why did you return to Rome?"

"There was something I could not reveal before," said Scipio. "I had no chance to do so at the curia. We survived the battle."

Servius leaned forward, and Scipio nodded.

"We survived. I'm not sure how, exactly. I was knocked unconscious from my horse, and a few hours later, was awakened by men from the Legio Votum and the XIV. Knowing that you were on your way to Rome, and with all of the confusion courtesy of Liberius, I figured I had better return to make a report to Majorian myself."

"How did we fare?" Servius asked.

"Rome deployed more than seven thousand men; fewer than eight hundred survived, every single one of them lightly wounded at least. Valerus, Decinius, and Modius were all killed. To be honest, I'm surprised as many lived as did. We're not alone. Sooner or later, word will reach Rome that we won a victory."

"And Rufus?"

"Escaped," Scipio said regretfully. "I am told that when the battle turned against him, he fled into the mountains. Eleven thousand Goths lay dead in the Aquilan Valley, plus those in the Aquilan Pass. Rufus's power is gone; his army is defeated. His confederation will dissolve."

"It's too bad the Senate didn't know of this," Servius said, shaking his head. His thoughts turned to Prisca, her soft hands, her glistening eyes, her gentle voice, her beauty... That was what he wanted... Not forums and speeches, not columns in the curia or columns on the battlefield... but a family... land... to work the earth, to draw forth the blessings of the land, the blessings of God.

"Oh, the Senate will find out, sooner or later," Scipio said. "And so will the people of Rome, when almost eight hundred men come limping back home, in victory nonetheless."

"I suppose," Servius mused, leaning his head back against the wall behind him, "that I would rather be vindicated in death, then be forced to live a lie."

"The Senate," Scipio acknowledged.

"It isn't a place for me... I can't be pragmatic the way that Orianus and Vespius can, though their hearts are in the right places. I can't be anything less than honest... Otherwise, I'm not being honest with myself, or God." Servius looked over at Scipio. "You didn't have to come back."

"I knew they would accuse you of desertion," Scipio said. "Beyond Liberius's machinations... There was no way I was going to let you stand alone." Scipio sat up straight. "So now that Rufus is dead, I can have something to drink."

Servius smirked. "In moderation."

"In moderation," confirmed Scipio. "Don't ask me to be moderate if I ever get the chance to go after Liberius."

"We won't even get the chance to," Servius said. "You know what public trials are like that are headed by corrupt men... They build crowds into frenzies... the crowds then condemn those on trial... and those on trial are executed by decapitation, if they are lucky. If not, they are turned loose to the crowds."

Scipio shook his head. "We're animals, aren't we?"

"A different kind of animal... We're separate from the wild for a reason... because of reason... because of our souls... But our minds and hearts don't always prevail over our natural passions."

From out in the passageway came the shuffle of feet, the presence of the prison guards, of the commandant of the imperial penitentiary. He came to the cell door, followed by several of his men.

"General Scipio, Senator Servius," the commandant said with reluctance, "I am to deliver you to the forum."

"Then so you must," Servius said, putting his arms through the bars of the cell to be chained. The commandant waved his hand.

"That won't be necessary until we're outside," he said. "I'm tired of seeing good men in this place. Walk out of here with honor."

With that, the door to the cell was opened, and the commandant moved down to the next pen, where Titus, Horatio, and the other guards who had accompanied Scipio back to Rome were being kept.

"So it is dawn," Servius said. "And so it is night."

XIV

The main forum before the curia was crowded with thousands, standing silently, somberly, looking on, waiting to see what it was that Liberius had to say. The public remembered well the incident on the Cassian Way at Aurelian Field, but they were familiar with Liberius, familiar with the power he held, familiar with his shrewd ways that, whatever the method, got things done —or so they were told. Now Liberius was set to try publicly Servius, Scipio, and a host of men declared deserters. Yet, rumors abounded: either there was a victory, pyrrhic, but still a victory —or there was a massacre, and Scipio and Servius had, in cowardice, saved their own skins.

Liberius's thugs stood about a raised platform, and the Roman Senate stood on the steps of the curia behind them. Cleander stood to the side, a smug look on his face, enjoying the periphery of center stage, enjoying the cusp of power without actually controlling it.

Liberius was absolutely enthralled, recognizing that the path of his return to unchecked supremacy in politics was at hand, through both the approach of Rufus, and the decimation of his greatest senatorial opposition.

Their hands shackled, Servius and Scipio were brought up onto the stage by Liberius's thugs, with Titus, Horatio, and the others brought up behind them. The crowd continued to be strangely silent, as though watching a dream unfold. Days before, they had cheered Servius and Scipio as heroes; now, their heroes were before them in chains like slaves or common criminals. The citizens of Rome were used to the duplicitous and corrupt nature of their leaders, but this was not an opinion many shared of the men who now stood above them.

Liberius wasted no time.

"Many of you may not know this about me, but I was born and raised in the northern reaches of Italy, where my father farmed the land and I grew to love the country and everything that Rome was. So it was no far cry that I should have conferred upon Senator Servius the authority to defend our country, out of the kindness and pang of my heart.

"The mission was simple. Servius and Scipio were to stop Rufus, to confront him, even though we had not yet exhausted all other peaceable means for resolution of the crisis. While we are still awaiting news of the battle that followed that of Aquilo, we do know for a fact that Servius and Scipio, as well as their aides, experienced a stunning and unprecedented streak of cowardice and abandoned their troops. These men are guilty of desertion. Rather than fight to the death as their own troops may well have done, Servius, upon whose shoulders alone the entire enterprise rested, chose to divest himself of his responsibilities and flee for his life."

There was some booing from the crowd, but no great outcry. Servius seethed, wanting to rush forward to topple Liberius from the platform, to countermand the charges, the lies. But there would be little use. He would be executed before the end of the day, with or without the public's approval. If Liberius commanded it, it would be so.

At the far end of the platform, a simple wooden crate —crude, but honest, and marked as formerly containing olives —was overturned beside one of Liberius's thugs, who himself held an axe. Servius realized that he would not live to see the afternoon.

"Now!" called Liberius, his voice resounding shrilly. "There is only one punishment for desertion! And that is execution!" There was more booing, but most of the audience remained passive. "The accused have refused to say anything at all in their defense, and their silence provides all the evidence needed! For what can a deserter say about cowardice? Nothing!"

Liberius turned to his men. "First, the senator." His voice was sadistically gleeful.

Servius was shoved forward, and he began the walk across the stage to the executioner, but a single voice rang out behind him.

"Wait!" said Scipio, stepping after the senator. "I will go first, that the senator may live a moment longer."

"And I," said Horatio.

"And I," added Titus.

"And we," said one of the other men who had ridden in with Scipio.

Liberius cackled. "I'm *touched*. I hope Servius will enjoy seeing his friends die."

"No," said Servius. "I will lead the way."

"This is, in itself, a battlefield," said Scipio solemnly. "I cannot allow that."

Without waiting for a response, the old general made his way across the platform, falling on his knees before the crate.

"I have made my peace with Christ," Scipio said. "And I am prepared to face whatever comes." He leant forward, his eyes closed, his heart and mind at peace, breathing slowly, deeply. The executioner, at Liberius's nod, raised high his axe.

"Stay your hand, criminal!"

The executioner barely had time to look to the direction of the voice. A single arrow impaled his chest and he fell back, dead. Liberius, Cleander, and their men brought their attention to the edge of the forum, where Orianus sat astride his horse, bow in hand. From behind him came the rumble of thunder, the resounding stamp of hoof.

Into the sunlight from the shadowed streets emerged Emperor Majorian, Prsica, Vespius, and the Emperor's Guards. The people in the forum cheered wildly, and the thugs on stage scattered like rats before the light. Liberius was stunned into immobility; Cleander took a few steps back; some of the Emperor's Guard began to climb the platform.

"What is the meaning of this!" shouted Majorian, fire in his eyes.

"M-m-my Lord," Cleander said, wringing his hands together.

"Silence!" Majorian commanded. "I was *not* talking to *you!*"

Servius breathed heavily, his heart lifting at the sight of Prisca as she moved toward the stage with the Emperor's men.

"The legions," Liberius squeaked out. "They have been defeated... Scipio... Servius... They were deserters..."

"That is a *lie!*" thundered Majorian. "Rufus has been *defeated* and the survivors of the battle are enroute back to Rome!"

"B-but that is *impossible!*" Liberius stammered.

"Traitor!" shouted someone in the audience toward Liberius.

"String him up!" shouted another.

"You betrayed our men," Majorian said in a deadly calm. "You were dealing with Rufus."

The Emperor's Guards were untying the imprisoned, and Prisca herself tore open the ropes which bound Servius's hands. They embraced, tears streaming down Prisca's face.

"I was almost too late," she said. "Thank God.. Thank God I got to the emperor on time..."

"Liberius!" shouted Majorian. "What do you have to say for yourself?"

Liberius said nothing, merely took a step back – only to find his shoulder gripped by Scipio, who proceeded to punch him across the face, knocking him off his feet.

"His silence is evidence!" Scipio yelled. The crowd surged in cheers as soldiers accosted Liberius. Cleander bolted, then, to escape, leaping from the stage, and tumbling over himself onto the ground, bloodying his hands. But the people of Rome were there, and they grabbed at him, preventing him from escaping, throwing him back to the stage and to the custody of the Emperor's Guard.

"Go and track down their hired men!" commanded Majorian of all the onlookers. "And bring them to the imperial prison for justice!"

With that, the Emperor's Guard and the people went off after the criminals that had fled. Emperor Majorian, followed by Orianus, Vespius, and several other Guards, then ascended the platform themselves. Liberius was picked up and held, as was Cleander.

"So," said Majorian, glaring at Liberius. "This is what Rome was to you... Not the end, but a means to an end. All this time, *you* were plotting *against us*. For years you have been selling us out because you sought to purchase the throne at the expense of your own honor. Rest assured though, that your terrific little gambit has cost you everything. Get these accursed *vermin* out of my sight."

At once, Liberius and Cleander were dragged away, with Cleander begging for mercy, that he had been an unwilling accomplice, that Majorian was just and wise and must spare him. Scipio patted Servius on the back.

"I told you I wouldn't be moderate with Liberius. I was hoping for a second shot, though."

Servius breathed in deeply. "Scipio," he said, holding tightly onto Prisca. "Thank you..."

"It's an honor," said Scipio, nodding to Majorian. "An honor." He then turned to Orianus. "You managed to keep your talent with bow, even after all these years?"

Orianus grinned.

"This man," Scipio said, pointing to Orianus, "was part of our legion's archery cohort twenty years ago."

"Some things never change," Orianus said.

"Well," Vespius confessed, wiping his brow. "I've been trapped in my room for the better part of a day, and I'm hungry. If you'll excuse me, I'm going to find a baker."

Majorian approached Servius and Prisca, his crimson robe fluttering in the spring breeze that swept in across the city that was eternal. "Senator," said the Emperor. "You have done extraordinary things. And so has this girl."

"She has," Servius agreed, his mind turning quickly to more pressing matters. "How are the new legions?"

"They're being raised," Majorian revealed. "Thanks to you." He paused a moment, thinking, considering his next words. He breathed in sharply. "Will you stay on in the Senate, despite all of this?"

Servius breathed in deeply, the images of home, of family, of quiet fleeting before him like morning shadows beneath the afternoon sunlight. The Emperor was calling him to continue serving, just the way that the Empire called upon its legions. A soldier didn't return home after only one battle.

"We'll stay," Prisca whispered. "I'll go wherever you'll go."

Servius kissed her forehead.

"Emperor Majorian," he said. "It appears as though we'll be in Rome for some time."

The Emperor gracefully bowed his head. And as the Emperor and his men withdrew, and as the crowds dissipated, only Servius and Prisca remained on the platform, her hair swept about her shoulder by the warm, spring wind. And Servius reached up and touched her face, softly, tenderly; and she put her hands on his neck, and they kissed.

"I think," Servius said, linking his arm in Prisca's, "that it's time we took a little time to ourselves. I think we should go and see Father Marcellus, and see what he has to say about marrying us. It's May, now… A new month… a new season is ahead."

ROME
After April, 458 A.D.

With his power secure, Emperor Majorian personally takes command of new legions and troops from allied tribes and nations, launching swift and stunning campaigns that reconquer most of Spain and Gaul, subduing rebellious tribes and crushing Rome's enemies. He implements many popular civil and religious reforms, and is greatly loved by the people. His plans to reconquer northern Africa from the Vandals come undone dramatically when traitors help to destroy the fleet being readied for the campaign.

In 461, Majorian's ablest general and supporter, the barbarian Ricimer, turns against him, fearing Majorian's power, and falsely accusing Majorian of indecisiveness. He has Majorian arrested, tortured, and beheaded. Ricimer then pushes another to the throne, signaling the final descent to collapse. Ricimer himself ultimately dies of a hemorrhage. The quick succession of emperors that follows, in conjunction with corrupt politics, culture, and external and internal threats, finally leads to the fall of the Western Roman Empire fifteen years later.

Upon his return to Gaul, Rufus's power is gone. His disastrous campaign in Italy has brought many enemies against him. He is captured by allies of Rome while attempting to flee to Germania, and is taken to Ravenna, where he is publicly executed before Roman citizens.

Liberius is stripped of his wealth and his estates, and condemned to the same fate he once condemned Scipio to. Liberius commits suicide shortly thereafter.

Cleander spends the next fifteen years in prison, and lives out his remaining years as a peasant farmer in Sicily.

Orianus and Vespius continue to serve in the Senate until Rome falls. Thereafter, both men return to their villas. Orianus is arrested for refusing to pay taxes to the Gothic emperor Odoacer, and is exiled to the East. Vespius spends several years on his villa, enduring the new Gothic rulers and their harsh reign, until he finally leaves for Greece.

Scipio goes on to serve alongside Majorian in the campaigns that reconstitute the Western Empire. He is killed in battle in Spain.

Servius and Prisca are ultimately married by Marcellus and have three children. Servius serves as senator until Majorian's death. When rumor spreads that Servius is being considered for the throne, Servius rejects the idea, and he and Prisca bring their young family back to northern Italy. But the instability following Majorian's death compels Servius to decide to move his family to the Eastern Empire, where he serves Emperor Leo I as a civil and military adviser for three years, and retires to farm and raise his family in Western Greece. There, Servius, Prisca, and their family happily live out their years.

ACKNOWLEDGMENTS

The first draft of this novel was completed in 2012, several years after it was first conceived. Interest in the Roman Empire is perpetual, and whether one comes down on the side of Rome, or the Empire's opponents or enemies, very much depends on the era, place, and culture. This is true of any period in history given the times in which those periods are considered, and it is often reflected in historiography and historical fiction.

At the time of writing of these ackonlwedgments (September 2014), the United States is in a situation quite similar to that of the late Western Roman Empire: we are faced with internal and external enemies of various kinds; and doubt, both in purpose and in position, have led to intense critical self-examination and the thought that perhaps the world might be better off without America leading it. I utterly reject this view, as is clear in the novel by way of the use of Rome as a metaphor. As the historian and writer Victor Davis Hanson once remarked, we have convinced ourselves as Americans that, because we aren't perfect, we cannot be good. Hanson and I both disagree with this idea. We are an intrinsically good people. You don't have to be perfect to be good –a point I brought out frequently by way of Servius.

Rome was by no means perfect, and was often outright brutal and unforgiving – a far cry from the United States. Yet the light that Rome brought to the world cannot be denied, especially in the later period of its history through the influence of Christianity, and the spread of Judeo-Christian ideas. Though Americans may lament the poor parts of our own history, that is no reason not to strive to be better, or to recognize the good that we have done, and continue to do in the world. There is no nation more giving, more generous, more sympathetic to the plights of others, both at home and abroad, than the United States. To say that we are this way simply because we can afford to be this way is nonsense. Americans are, by and large, simply good-hearted people.

This novel came about by way of seeking to address particular contemporary issues by way of historical metaphor and fiction, to demonstrate that it is never too late to turn things around, and to reinforce and explore the idea that a few good people can make a difference no matter how late the hour. In such moments, heroes do step forward —such as Aetius, who battled Attila the Hun, and Majorian, who essentially reconstituted most of the Western Empire within a few short years. Yet, tragically, such heroes are often undermined or torn down for various reasons, mostly of corruption and power-playing at the very moments they are needed most. The United States has no shortage of such men and women, known and unknown, at the moment: they simply need to be supported, and not opposed. That doesn't just go for politics, but for everyday life as well. Our fate as a nation is still in our hands. As Ronald Reagan believed in the 1980s, and as Americans must still believe now —our best days are still ahead of us. Yet it is up to each and every single one of us, with God's guidance, to make that possible.

A number of people have helped make this novel possible, by their encouragement and support. I want to thank God, first and foremost, for giving me life and the ability to love and write. I very much want to thank my mother, Valerie Bouthyette, whose endless love and encouragement have helped to sustain me. I want to thank my stepfather, Pierre Bouthyette, an absolutely erudite man with whom I have had no shortage of discussion about American politics and Roman history – and where the two intersect. I want to thank my father, Ray Vigliotti, whose common sense and straightforward considerations of current events are invaluable, for his support and encouragement as well.

I want to thank FutureWord Publishing, headed up by the wonderful Cheryl Haynes, who is herself an incredible friend and writer, and provides unrelenting form of support.

I want to thank two of my best friends, Ian Eppig and Tyler Barnes, for always having my back and always reading the things I have written. I also wish to thank numerous other friends, including Maryland State Representative Justin Ready, Jessica Smith, and Karen Lonaberger, all for their encouragements and feedback on the novel.

And I especially want to thank *you*, for taking the time to have read this. The point of writing is so that it can be read, which makes all the difference.

JOE VIGLIOTTI is the author of the award-winning novel *Carnival Week*, and several other books. A native of Long Island, New York, he now resides in Maryland. He can be reached through his website at www.jvigliotti.com

Books by Joe Vigliotti:

Cross of the Confederacy (2007)

Carnival Week (2010)

Return to the Shore (2010)

One May Weekend (2013)

A Rose in February (2013)

Ghosts on the Tower (2013)

The Sea in the Sky (2014)

Made in the USA
Middletown, DE
15 August 2016